Howl of the West

I want to dedicate this to everyone who believed in it; you
know who you are!

Chapter 1

Get the Hell Out of Dodge

Clive Holiday is a wanted man, and the crime he is wanted for is murder. The relatively quiet and welcoming town of Dodge City, unless you cheated a fellow gambler in the local saloon, was the scene of the crime. Clive hadn't meant to kill anyone; it was supposed to be a routine shakedown.

The folks of Dodge City have been on edge lately, as their cattle are turning up dead. *Dead* wasn't even the right word, *mangled* was closer to the truth. With the townspeople's primary source of income under threat, suspicion grew. Could it be those damn coyotes? Or was it something more sinister, like rival ranchers trying to "take out the competition"?

"You mess with a man's way of livin', don't be surprised if you're pushin' up daisies," was the ranchers' mentality.

Dodge City had once been a quiet place, somewhere a small rancher could settle down and make an honest living. In many ways, it still was if you could find work as a rancher or farmer. It wasn't because the economy was failing; in fact, it was thriving. The real problem was that older ranchers, who had been comfortable before the boom, now found it more challenging to compete. Some left town to seek work elsewhere, while others turned to less honorable pursuits.

Men like Clive, who had spent their whole lives as the heartbeat of Dodge City, felt abandoned while the city kept moving forward. What gave these new faces the right to come in and push them out? After all, they had given everything they had to the people of Dodge City. Were they truly unjustified in trying to reclaim what they believed was owed to them? They didn't think so.

"Empty your pockets!" Clive demanded, pointing his revolver at the man in front of him. Usually, that was enough to strike fear, but this day was different. The innocent man being held up for his money decided he wasn't going to give in without a fight. When the chance came, he lunged at Clive, fighting with everything he had to wrestle the gun away. Within seconds, the scene shifted from shouting and struggling to a single, thunderous *bang*, then silence. But even that silence didn't last. It was broken by blood-curdling screams from the surrounding crowd.

Why did he have to try to be a hero? Clive thought, spurring his horse as fast as it would go, desperate to outrun the sheriff and his posse of lawmen. The victim's face was now forever etched into Holiday's mind. One moment, the man had been going about his day; the next, his lifeless eyes stared up at the sky, blood pooling beneath him, all for some money and a cheap silver pocket watch. The life of an outlaw hadn't always been in the cards for Clive. More ranchers meant more competition, and more competition meant less demand for Clive's services, not to mention the town being terrorized by something prowling in the night. So what quicker way to make cash than to hold up unsuspecting folks? It had never turned violent, that is, until now.

"Stop! You're under arrest!" the lawmen shouted, also on horseback, not far behind the outlaw.

The scorching July heat meant Clive's horse couldn't run forever. He needed a plan, and he needed one fast. One mile turned into two, and then his prayers were answered. In the distance, the loud blow of a train's whistle cut through the air. Clive knew his only way out was to reach that train or face the hangman's rope.

"Come on, faster, faster!" Clive yelled at his horse, glancing back as the posse fired their rifles into the air. If the weight of his life hanging in the balance didn't make him faint, the heat might. With the lawmen closing in, Clive pressed alongside the train, stood on his horse, and barely caught his balance before leaping. Gripping the side of the train car, the fugitive hauled himself up as bullets whistled past, missing him by inches.

After following the train for some distance, the sheriff and his crew eventually gave up. Clive Holiday didn't know where the train was headed. What he did know was that he was a wanted man, and if caught, he'd be found guilty and hanged—if the victim's family didn't get to him first. Wherever the train was going, Clive was along for the ride.

As the train rattled on, night began to settle in, and the blanket of darkness seemed endless. Fading in and out of restless sleep, Clive kept reaching into his jacket to make sure his score was safe: one hundred fifty-seven dollars.

"And they say crime doesn't pay," he muttered with a smirk.

"Heh-heh-heh," a bellowing cackle rose from behind a stack of boxes on the other side of the car. "I've never heard that one before," a raspy voice said.

"W-W-Who's there? Come out!" the fugitive demanded, his gun drawn and aimed into the darkness.

From behind the boxes stepped a sharply dressed man, illuminated only by the full moon shining through the clear night sky. He wore what looked like his Sunday best, complete with a bowler hat perched on his head. It made no sense why a man who looked like he had money would be hiding on a train. With his arms raised, the stranger inched closer to the outlaw.

"My name is Ed. Do you always meet new people with a gun pointed at them?"

"Depends. Do you always lurk around in the shadows, waiting to sneak up on people?" the outlaw retorted, cocking the hammer of his revolver. "Why is a man like you hiding on a train?"

"Well, to be honest, I'm doing the same thing you're doing, running from the law. I guess that makes us one and the same. So why don't you lower the gun and tell me your name, friend?" Ed said with a chuckle, lowering his hands, but not too fast; he didn't want the outlaw to make a hasty decision with his gun.

"I never said I was running from the law, and need you no mind what my name is," the outlaw said, growing visibly angrier.

"You didn't have to tell me you were hiding from the law. I've been hopping trains for years and have seen countless men like you. I know you, once were you: your dirty, torn-up clothes, the reek of cheap booze. We may not look alike, but I find it easier to steal from and cheat the common folk if you look even a little trustworthy, a wolf in sheep's clothing, if you will. I gotta tell you, the money I've spent on these nice clothes is mere pennies compared to what I swindle out of people because of them. All I have to do is walk into a bank, slip the teller a note, and I'm gone before the sheriff can even stand up at the office. You aren't even allowed near the bank and still have to resort to petty theft at saloons," Ed explained, beaming with pride.

Clive didn't know if he was more impressed or pissed off at the thought of someone being better at his game than himself. He'd put years into honing what he called his "craft," holding up countless stagecoaches and passersby. After all, one hundred fifty-seven dollars might last him a few weeks, but after that, he'd have to hunt for his next big score, putting his neck on the line again and risking the rest of his miserable days behind bars. Maybe they'd show him some leniency, given that all but one of his robberies hadn't ended in blood. But who was Clive fooling? He was going to hang, and he knew it.

He noticed, though, that Ed wasn't acting like a man with a revolver pointed at him. He seemed relaxed.

"Tell me, how much did you pull in from your last job?" Ed asked, amused, knowing the answer wouldn't be enough by his standards.

"About two hundred dollars," Clive answered, rounding up to bolster his ego.

Ed leaned in, never breaking eye contact with the outlaw, "What if I told you I could double it and all you'd have to do is play a little game with me?"

Clive lowered his gun, intrigued by the prospect of doubling his money. After a moment's thought, he replied, "What's the catch?"

"Catch? Well, there is no catch. But I will say I have yet to lose," Ed said with a little pep in his step.

Reaching into the interior pocket of his expensive dress jacket, the man pulled out three playing cards. "Make yourself useful and drag one of those boxes over, will ya," he said. Once Clive dragged the box over, Ed laid the three cards face down. "The game is Three-Card Monte. All you have to do is find the ace."

Clive thought the game seemed simple enough. "Thirty seconds to double my money?" he asked.

"That's all it takes. But once the game is over, that's it, no do-overs and no funny business," Ed explained.

After shuffling the cards on the table, it was now up to Clive to make his choice. With his heart racing a mile a minute, he decided on the card directly in the middle. After all, there was no way he could lose; he was positive he'd kept his eyes locked on the ace the whole time. He pointed to the center card, and after a slight hesitation, Ed turned it over.

"Oh! Two of hearts. That's too bad," Ed said, an ever-so-slight hint of joy in his tone. And just like that, Clive lost everything. All one hundred fifty-seven dollars went up in smoke right in front of him. Everything he'd gone through was for nothing. The poor man Clive had shot in cold blood for nothing. All he had left now were empty pockets on a train he had no idea where it was headed.

"You hustled me. Give me back my money!" Clive shouted in a fit of rage.

"Hustle you? Did I not warn you that I have never lost? I never said you had to play the game. It ain't my fault you're so consumed by greed you can't use common sense. That's the problem with men like you, never giving a second thought to the consequences of your actions, only when things go south. And then you stand there with the audacity—"

Before Ed had time to finish his rant, *BANG!* Clive yanked the revolver from his gun belt and shot Ed square in the chest.

Consumed with fury, Clive walked over to the wounded man and stood above him, studying him. His once-expensive suit jacket was now stained with blood, and his bowler hat lay on the floor of the train car. The man was dead.

Without thinking twice, Clive reached into Ed's pocket and snatched back his money. But after searching further, he realized the man carried no cash at all, confirming Clive's suspicion that he'd been hustled.

Clive slumped down in the corner of the train, the weight of it all pressing on him. Among the rattling cargo, there was now nothing but an outlaw and a dead man.

Chapter 2

The Beast Is Unleashed

The train rolled on into the night as Clive sat slumped against the wall of the car. Two dead in less than twenty-four hours. This wasn't who he was, but he knew it didn't matter.

"They'll hang me for sure," he whispered, holding his head in his hands. A heartless man, Clive was not. He was, as his mother used to say, a victim of happenstance. He hadn't meant to shoot the man back in Dodge City, and the man on the train had stolen his money. In Clive's mind, he hadn't been given a choice. By now, the weight of it all had him so distraught that tears welled in his eyes. Across the car lay Ed's body, still and cold.

"I had no choice!" he screamed at the corpse. "Why did you make me do this?" His voice cracked as he shouted at the lifeless form.

"We all have a choice," a faint whisper muttered back.

"Who said that?" Clive snapped, standing up as fast as he could, and drew his gun. "Come on out. Show yourself."

But nothing stirred. Just the clatter of the train wheels.

Clive let out a shaky breath and reached into his jacket for his flask. He stared at it for a moment. Cheap whiskey burned more than it comforted, but it sure wasn't strong enough to make a man hear voices. Still, he took another swig.

He stumbled, lost his footing, and fell back against the boards, landing beside the body.

"How did I let things get this bad?" he muttered aloud. "I did everything I was supposed to. And when times were good… they were good. But now look at me, on the run from the law and talking to a corpse."

"You know, I didn't ask for Dodge City to become such a hotspot for ranchers. I mean, I was there first, long before these other followers came along and stole all my business. All those people are sheep, just mindlessly following the pack. They see a hardworking man like myself bust his tail, not only making a name for himself, but putting his town on the map as the number one spot for ranchers, and then they push him out. Instead of coming up with an original idea in their empty heads, those sheep stole mine and left me penniless," Clive said to the corpse resentfully.

"Like sheep to the slaughter," a voice said.

Clive jumped again, frightened by the voices.

"We all have a choice. Like sheep to the slaughter. We all have a choice. Like sheep to the slaughter," the voice kept repeating.

"Stop it!" Clive pleaded.

"Stop it? Did the man back in Dodge City get the chance to tell you to stop before you shot him dead? How about poor me? I didn't even have time to think before you put a bullet in me," the voice said.

"Me? What… what do you mean by me?" Clive asked, desperation clear in his voice.

The voice went back to chanting: "We all have a choice. Like sheep to the slaughter. We all have a choice. Like sheep to the slaughter."

"STOP! PLEASE!" Clive cried in hysterics.

Clive paced back and forth as if trying to outrun the voice. He pressed his hands over his ears in a desperate attempt to block it out, but it didn't work. The voice only grew louder.

"WE ALL HAVE A CHOICE! LIKE SHEEP TO THE SLAUGHTER! WE ALL HAVE A CHOICE! LIKE SHEEP TO THE SLAUGHTER!"

Clive, crying now, reached into his gun belt and pulled out his revolver. He pointed it straight up and fired. *BANG!*

Just like that, the voice went from yelling to silence. Clive dropped to the floor in exhaustion next to the dead man.

"I guess if they catch me and make me stand trial in Dodge City, I can claim insanity," Clive said in a failed attempt to lighten the situation and make himself feel better.

"Heh-heh-heh," a familiar cackle came from right next to Clive.

Clive looked down at Ed's lifeless body lying there. "There ain't no way," he said out loud.

A low moan escaped, and just like that, Ed's body began to rise slowly. In a pool of his own blood, he stood staring at Clive, the wound in his chest still leaking onto his vest and dress shirt. Ed walked behind a few boxes where his bowler hat lay, dusted it off, and placed it back on his head as he returned to Clive.

"You ruined my nice shirt," Ed said in an annoyed tone.

Unable to process what he was seeing, Clive could only stammer, "Y-Y-Y–"

"Come on, let it out," Ed encouraged.

"Y-Y-You w-w-were dead. I-I-I shot you," Clive finally managed.

"That's right, you did shoot me. Why did you do that?" Ed asked.

Clive, getting back to his feet, replied, "Because you swindled me."

"Swindled you? I did no such thing. I gave you fair warning that I have never lost at Three-Card Monte. It wasn't my fault that all you cared about was doubling your money. Just like the men before you, you were blinded by greed. I may not know your name, but I know you just as well as you know yourself. There's an old saying that jealousy is a green-eyed monster, but I believe greed is a far more dangerous, savage beast. What is it you said? They say crime doesn't pay? That may be true, but you, my friend, certainly will," Ed explained. It was at that moment that Ed fell to the ground in what could only be described as a seizure, letting out harrowing screams that pierced the night. All Clive could do was stare in horror. Ed contorted in unnatural ways, and his eyes, once green, had turned a yellowish-red. Claws tore through the skin of his hands and feet, formerly encased in the finest shoes Clive had ever seen, now replaced by paw-like extremities. His average-looking face elongated into a snout-like structure.

As he screamed, his mouth revealed teeth now replaced with razor-sharp fangs. Ed's once-pristine dress shirt tore as his spine pierced through the back of it. Standing upright, covered in hair and frothing at the mouth, he let out a howl that could wake the dead.

Chapter 3

A Helping Hand

"What the—" Clive could barely get the words out. The beast began walking toward him, growling and snarling. Clive reached for his gun belt and pulled out his revolver, firing a shot that hit the beast in the shoulder. The creature let out an angry roar. It swung at Clive, catching his arm and cutting him.

The beast wound up for another attack, but Clive ducked under the swing and ran to the other end of the train car. In a desperate move, he threw a couple of boxes at the man-beast, hoping to create some distance.

Dodging further attacks, Clive found his back against the opening of the train car. With his revolver aimed at the beast, he pulled the trigger. *BANG!* Just as he fired, the beast swiped one of its paws at him, sending Clive flying backward off the train, but not before the bullet struck the creature, making it yelp in pain.

The train rolled on with the beast wounded, while Clive lay unconscious beside the tracks. Fading in and out of consciousness, Clive awoke the next day in a strange twin-sized bed, surrounded by unfamiliar furnishings. A frail elderly man knocked on the doorframe.

"Good, you're awake. You gave us quite the scare," he said.

"Where am I? Did I kill it?" Clive asked.

"Kill what?" the man inquired.

"The beast... it was huge, had razor-sharp teeth, and was covered in hair. I-I-It looked like a wolf," Clive explained.

"Whoa, whoa, whoa! You hit your head pretty hard and knocked yourself out cold. And it's a good thing we found you when we did, because it looked like you were going to bleed out from the gash on—"

"THE BEAST!" Clive yelled.

"Now listen here!" Paul's voice grew stern as he stomped his cane on the ground. "It's just me and my wife out here, and I will not have you scaring her with your tall tales of beasts and monsters. I've spent sixty-eight years on this earth without hearing talk of monsters except in books. We think logically here. The reality is, yes, you were probably attacked by a wolf. There are plenty of those bastards running around, killing livestock and attacking innocent folk. You just don't want to be caught outside alone without your rifle. You can stay until you're back on your feet, but no more talk of monsters. Understood?" Paul said.

Clive shook his head in agreement.

"The name's Paul Kelp. How about we start with you telling me your name as well?" Paul asked.

"Clive," he responded.

Paul studied Clive for a moment, eyebrows furrowed. "You have a last name, Clive?"

Looking down at his bandaged arm, Clive replied, "Just Clive."

"Say, Paul, not to be rude, but you don't look much like the type who can close a wound this well," Clive chuckled.

"Well, just Clive, don't let my looks fool ya. I'm actually the town doctor and a fine one at that, if I do say so myself. When you're back up and running again, you should come on down and check it out. That being said, I'm burning daylight and have to open the clinic. If you get bored, there's plenty to read, and if you get hungry, there's stew on the table. I should be back before sundown."

As Paul walked out of the room, Clive perked up. "You said it was just you and your wife living here?"

Paul stopped at the doorframe, turned around, and replied, "That's right, and we took your gun just to be safe. You never know what type of folks you can run into out there. I put the money that was in your pocket in the nightstand drawer to your right. We're not in the business of stealing working folks' money. Also, your pocket watch is in there as well. I figured you couldn't do much damage with that. As for my wife, Susan, you'll meet her soon enough, but she's feeling under the weather, so she'll be locked in her room for the day. If you could try to keep the noise to a minimum, that would be appreciated. The last thing I ask is that you please stay out of the tool shed."

"May I ask why?" Clive asked.

With a deadpan expression, Paul said, "Just don't."

After Paul left the room, Clive waited for the front door to shut before pulling himself out of bed and walking toward the window. He watched as Paul mounted his horse and rode off toward town. Clive stood there for a while longer, staring at the tool shed.

"What could possibly be in there?" he asked himself.

Throughout the day, Clive explored the house. He walked every square inch of the property. The Kelps had a small chicken coop outside, and Clive watched the chickens cluck around for about thirty minutes, just trying to burn some time. In his peripheral vision to his right, the tool shed stood there, luring him in. He walked over to it and pulled on the door handle, but the entrance was chained shut.

Whatever was in there certainly wasn't for public knowledge.

Inside, Clive came across a locked room. He assumed it was where Susan was resting. He knocked on the door three times.

Knock... Knock... Knock.

"Mrs. Kelp, are you in there?"

No answer.

"Mrs. Kelp, is there anything I can get you?"

Still no answer. Clive shrugged and proceeded to explore the house.

As the day rolled on, Clive found himself getting increasingly bored. He walked to the bookshelf inside and started perusing mostly tales of cowboys and pioneers until one title stood out: *Myths and Legends Bestiary*. He flipped through the pages, looking at diagrams of vampires and the elusive Bigfoot, each accompanied by brief descriptions.

"Bullshit," Clive scoffed.

He flipped through pages, finding them increasingly more amusing, his favorites being the sea monster and the Yeti. He let out an audible chuckle until he turned the page and saw something that made his blood run cold. There, staring back at him, was a diagram of the monster that attacked him on the train. It looked exactly like it, from the claws to the razor-sharp teeth. Next to the frightening diagram, it read:

"The werewolf only shows its true self under the pale moonlight. It takes the form of a regular human during the day. The only way to kill a werewolf is by destroying the entire body or with a silver bullet to the heart."

"Silver bullet? I've only ever heard of lead bullets," Clive whispered to himself.

As the day rolled on, Clive lay in bed with the intention of resting up, feeling vindicated, knowing that what he saw last night was real. He was in that state between not being fully awake and not completely asleep when he swore he heard rattling from the chains on the shed door. He got up in his half-dream state and walked out to the shed. Clive tried to pull as hard as he could on the door to no avail. He walked to a line of rocks that marked the end of the Kelps' property. Clive retrieved a rock and proceeded to try to break it. In the distance, he could hear the galloping of what could only be Paul's horse.

"Shit!" Clive said, throwing the rock as far as he could to destroy the evidence.

Clive quietly ran into the house and lay back in bed. He heard a knock on his bedroom doorframe.

"How ya feeling?" Paul asked.

"Like I've been hit by a train," Clive replied.

Paul chuckled. "Did you eat the stew I left for you on the table?"

Clive shook his head.

"How do you expect to get your strength back if you refuse to eat? Anyway, I have some chores to do before the sun completely sets, but when I come back, we can reheat the grub and have supper. If you could do me a favor and start the fire in the wood stove in the kitchen, so it's ready to go. If you need more firewood, it's behind the house," Paul explained.

Clive replied, "Of course."

So off they went. Paul attended to the chickens while Clive gathered the firewood. In search for matches, Clive found them on the windowsill above the sink. As he grabbed them, he peered through the window and saw Paul unlocking the tool shed. Clive knelt down, hidden from view but able to see what the old man was doing.

Clive muttered to himself, "What are you doing in there, old timer?"

Clive proceeded to light the wood stove and poured the stew from the bowl on the table back into the pot. After about an hour, he heard the shed door open and hurried back to the window. By this point, the sun had completely set, and Paul was holding a lantern, casting light only on him and a small path in front of him. Clive watched him walk over to the chicken coop, pick up one of the chickens, and carry it back to the shed. He opened the door slightly, released the chicken inside, closed the door behind him, locked it, and headed back toward the house.

The two sat down for supper, and Clive asked, "Will Mrs. Kelp be joining us this evening?"

"No, sorry. She is far too under the weather to join us," the old man replied.

"Hey, Clive, you never told me what you did for work," Paul said.

Clive, not looking up from his bowl of stew, replied, "I am a rancher in Dodge City, well, I used to be."

"What do you mean you were a rancher in Dodge City? Did something happen?" Paul asked.

Clive looked up from his bowl, locking eyes with the elderly man. "I was doing well for myself until word got out about how good business was in Dodge City. Before I knew it, there were at least two competing ranchers in the same town as me. Two eventually turned into three, and the more ranchers there were, the less money came in."

"Dodge City is a way north. What are you doing all the way down here in the small town of Moonlight Valley?" Paul asked.

Lying through his teeth, Clive answered, "Well, you see, after work dried up, I decided to hop the train and take it wherever it stopped. I know what you're thinking, why didn't I just take my horse? I sold it for some extra cash. Unfortunately, my story doesn't go much farther than that, and I slipped and fell off the train. That's where you found me."

In between slurping his stew, Paul quietly asked, "And your arm?"

"Wolves. Don't want to be caught outside alone with them, you said so yourself," Clive answered with a smirk, remembering that if he brought up beasts or monsters, Paul would kick him out.

"Hahaha, when I found you, you were rambling on and on about monsters and nonsense. I thought you might have been hitting that flask we found on you a little too hard," Paul joked.

"Alright, that's enough about me. What about you? Have you been practicing medicine for a long time in… what did you call it? Moonlight Valley?"

"Yes and no," Paul said in his old voice, pausing between bites. He wiped his mouth and added, "I have been practicing medicine for close to forty years, but we moved here about three months ago. We actually hail from the east, but our old brittle bones can't do another winter out there. So, Susan and I set off west, knowing there would be no shortage of need for a doctor."

As dinner came to an end, Paul collected the dishes and brought them to the sink, while Clive carried a lantern and a bucket out to the nearby pond to fetch water. While he was outside, he could have sworn he heard low grunts from the shed, but he tried his best to ignore them. He knew he couldn't check it out anyway, since Paul was at the sink and the kitchen window faced directly toward the shed. Clive made his way back into the house, already planning how he might break in.

"Hey, why don't I come into town with you tomorrow instead of sitting around here all day?" Clive suggested, closing the front door behind him.

"I mean, you can definitely come and get acquainted with the town. I'll warn you, though, I'm pretty busy down at the office. More patients than ever before. But I wouldn't worry; nothing appears to be contagious," Paul replied.

Clive nodded in agreement, but he kept glancing out the front window as if something might jump out of the darkness. The rest of the night passed in silence until they both retired for the evening.

Chapter 4

A Different Kind of Sickness

"It's 8 o'clock, time to wake up," Paul said, poking an unresponsive Clive. "Come on now, I don't have much life left, and I can't spend it waiting on you."

Clive awoke from his slumber and sat up. "Okay, okay, old timer, I'm awake. Watch where you're putting that cane."

"Good. We leave in fifteen minutes, and I made coffee. Heaven knows I can't get through the day without it."

After Clive finished getting ready, he opened the nightstand. Staring back at him was the hundred fifty-seven dollars and that old silver pocket watch, the same blood money that had been the root cause of his unfortunate departure from Dodge City. He stared at it for a moment, remembering the poor man's face he had killed, before finally snapping to and shoving them into his pocket.

The men finished getting ready, and just as they were about to head out the door, Clive suggested, "Should we check if Susan needs anything before we leave?"

Paul stared at Clive over his glasses. "I already did before I woke you up. Just because you want to sleep the day away doesn't mean the rest of us don't have things to do. Now, if you're done chit-chatting, you'll be taking my wife's horse into town."

The two began saddling up the horses, and all the while, Clive could not take his eyes off the tool shed.

"Is there something interesting over there?" Paul asked.

"If I can ask, what exactly is in the tool shed?"

"Tools," Paul said flatly.

With that, the two set off toward town. The sun was out, but clouds in the distance threatened an overcast. They rode their horses in silence, giving Clive time to think. He couldn't quite put his finger on the old man. Paul had been kind enough to take him in, but anytime Clive tried to ask about anything personal, the old man snapped at him. Maybe it was Susan who had convinced her husband to bring home an unconscious stranger and nurse him back to health. But that didn't explain why Clive hadn't seen or even heard her.

When they arrived in town, Clive noticed a sign welcoming everyone to Moonlight Valley. The town had all the fixtures he had come to expect, having grown up in Dodge City. The odd part about this particular town was that the train ran right through the center, as if the town had been intentionally built around it. On one side of the tracks stood the saloon, the epicenter of nightlife, the post office, and the jail. On the other side were the general store, the blacksmith, and the doctor's office. Not exactly a booming metropolis.

There were also houses scattered along the outskirts on both sides of the tracks, but many of them had their windows and doors boarded shut. Clive didn't pay much attention to that detail, though. The town reminded him a lot of Dodge City, except here he was nobody. He wasn't wanted for murder. He didn't have to lie, cheat, or swindle. Here, he could start anew.

As the two approached the clinic, they hitched their horses out front.

As Paul proceeded to see patients, Clive went exploring the quiet town of Moonlight Valley. He walked into the saloon, sat down at the bar, and ordered a shot of whiskey.

"Haven't seen you around here. Just passing through?" the barkeep asked.

"No, actually staying with a friend. You may know him, his name is Paul Kelp."

"Doctor Kelp? Didn't know he had any friends. I've only ever seen him by himself."

"Clive," he said, reaching out his hand to shake the barkeep's. "Not even with his wife?" Clive pressed.

"I mean, I saw her the first day they arrived in town. But when more and more of the townsfolk started to get sick,

Doctor Kelp said he sent her to live with a relative back out east. He claimed he was afraid, with her being elderly and all, that she might catch whatever's being passed around Moonlight Valley."

Clive sat there in shock. The whole time he'd been at the Kelps', Paul had been lying to him. And if Paul had lied about Susan, then who was locked in that room back at the house, or, more importantly, what was hidden in the tool shed?

"What can you tell me about this sickness going around?" Clive asked, signaling for a refill on his whiskey.

"It's the oddest thing. One minute, just a few of the locals were sick, and now there isn't a day that I don't see a line of patients outside the doc's office."

A look of concern grew over Clive's face.

"You alright?"

"Yeah, I just realized I had something to do back at Paul's place. Say, do you think the general store carries any tools?"

"I mean, it's got a few things to fix up around the house. But if you're looking for farm equipment, you're gonna have to do some traveling."

"Just some repairs for the old man. Thank you kindly."

Clive quickly paid for his drinks and left in a hurry. As he passed by the line of locals outside Paul's practice, he noticed they didn't look sick at all. It struck him as strange that so many seemingly healthy folks were seeking medical attention.

He pressed on, moving past the town's blacksmith toward the general store. Bursting through the door so fast, he might have knocked it off its hinges if it hadn't been open.

"Where's the fire?" the clerk said.

"A thousand pardons. I'm just looking for some tools to fix up my chicken coop back home. Wouldn't want them getting out and getting snatched up by something."

"No worries at all," the clerk replied. "Tools are in the back of the store."

The entire time Clive searched for what he needed, the clerk never took his eyes off him. Maybe it was because Clive had barreled through the door like a madman, or maybe it was the lingering stench of whiskey on his breath.

"Just passing through?" the clerk asked.

"No. Nice little town you got here. I think I might be staying for a while."

"Well, welcome to Moonlight Valley. The name's Colt."

"Well, Colt, I don't mean to be rude, but I'm kinda in a hurry if you don't mind."

Clive bought the hammer, gave the clerk a respectful nod, and went on his way. Once outside, he slipped the hammer's handle into his trousers and pulled his coat closed to hide it, at least until he got back to his horse and could tuck it into the saddlebag.

The rest of the day, Clive lingered around the outside of Paul's office, just burning daylight. He made small talk with a few townsfolk, but when the sun began to set, the streets emptied. Not a soul lingered outside. Everyone was either across the way in the saloon or shut inside their homes, doing God knows what.

"You ready to go?" Paul asked, shutting and locking the door behind him.

"I saw all the town had to offer within the first hour, so yeah, I think I'm good."

The two set off for home.

"Say, Paul, why didn't most of the patients waiting to see you today look ill?"

"Well, sickness isn't just pneumonia or the flu, you see. I also have to treat the sicknesses you can't see."

"The sicknesses you can't see?"

"That's right. Let's take you, for example. Just by looking at you, you seem perfectly healthy. But if you roll up your sleeve, you reveal a nasty gash on your arm. Then there's sickness of the mind. A lot of those folks can't sleep due to insomnia, so I have to prescribe them something to help."

"And what would the fine folks of Moonlight Valley have to be stressed about?" Clive chuckled.

"Hey, young man, don't joke about those folks suffering. You have no clue what's going on in their lives. They're hardworking people, and most of them have fallen on hard times."

The two finished the ride home in silence, returning just before sundown. Clive headed inside while Paul did his nightly chores. From the kitchen window, Clive once again watched as Paul fed the chickens. Then, to Clive's unease, Paul picked one up and carried it into the shed. Clive knew that tonight had to be the night he found out what was inside.

The two once again sat down for another stew dinner, Clive once more noting the absence of Mrs. Kelp.

"Mrs. Kelp still feeling under the weather?"

"Yes," Paul quickly replied, not even looking up from his food.

"Do you think some fresh air might do her good? It can't be helping her to stay locked away in that back room all day and night."

"I'm sorry, I wasn't aware we had another doctor in the house. Where was it again you learned medicine?"

Clive stumbled over his words. "A-All I was trying to say is—"

"No, all you were trying to do was tell me how to run my household. All I've done is give you a place to stay until you heal up. In return, I asked only that you respect my privacy and stay out of our family business. So, for the last time, can you do that?"

Clive nodded and apologized.

"Good. Now finish your food and clean up because we have another early day tomorrow."

The rest of the night passed in silence. Clive did the dishes and then headed to his room with no intention of going to bed. He waited for the sound of Paul's door shutting, then sat in the dark, staring at his pocket watch. He counted down the minutes, waiting an hour before making his move.

Once that tarnished old silver pocket watch struck eleven o'clock, he knew the coast was clear. Opening his bedroom door as gently as he could, Clive slipped into the hallway, tiptoed through the kitchen, and slipped out the front door, lantern in hand to light his way.

Outside, he glanced back at the house one last time before running to Susan's horse. Reaching into the saddlebag, he pulled out the hammer. After one last deep exhale, he turned toward the tool shed.

WACK! Clive hit the lock on the shed as hard as he could. He looked back at the house, making sure the noise didn't wake the old man. *WACK!* The lock rattled.

"Come on, you lousy piece of—"

WACK! WACK! WACK! Clive kept at the lock until he suddenly felt something pressing into his back.

"Alright, that's enough! You just couldn't leave well enough alone, could you? Now drop that hammer and turn around slowly," the old man said, the barrel of his rifle jammed against Clive's back.

Clive raised his hands and turned slowly, showing he wasn't a threat. "There's something strange going on here," he said. "You've been lying to me about everything since I woke up."

"Lying about what?" Paul asked, gun still trained on him.

"Your wife. You said she was sick, that's why I've never seen her. But the bartender at the saloon told me you sent her to live with relatives so she wouldn't get sick from whatever's going around town."

Paul cocked the gun. "You don't go poking around a man's family business, Clive. I rescued you, brought you here, and this is how I'm repaid? I guess no good deed goes unpunished, as they say. So, tell me, son, what is it you want from me?"

"The truth!"

"How about you first."

"What are you talking about?"

The elderly man pressed the gun into Clive's chest. "I'll tell you what, I'm gonna make a deal with you. I know you're lying about what happened in Dodge City, because no honest man goes from being a rancher to a train-jumper unless he's running from something. So the deal is simple: you tell me the truth, and I'll tell you the truth."

Clive began to explain the events in Dodge City, how he'd gone from being an honest rancher to a life of crime. Paul stared at him in shock and dismay.

"You had us break the law by letting you stay here? You put not only my life, but my wife's in danger by letting a murderer play us for fools. I oughta end your miserable existence right here," Paul said, raising the barrel of the rifle to eye level with Clive.

"It was a mistake. I know one day my time will come to pay this debt for my sins, and I know I won't be able to."

"A mistake?" Paul questioned. "We're not talking about accidentally forgetting to take dinner off the stove so it burns. You took a man's life! It doesn't get much worse than that."

"I know, and I can't express how sorry I am."

The two stood there in silence for a moment. Nothing but dead air between them, yet somehow it was deafening.

Clive was the first to break the silence, "Alright, I lived up to my end of the agreement. Now it's your turn."

Paul continued to stare at him.

"Come on, a deal's a deal."

With one swift movement, Paul lowered his gun, and there was a sudden *BANG!* Clive's ears rang from the gunshot. He looked back at the shed and saw the stubborn lock lying on the ground. It took Clive a minute to gather his composure, then he turned back to Paul, who jabbed at him with the rifle, forcing him toward the shed.

"Go on, turn around and open it," Paul demanded. "You wanted the truth? Well, the truth is behind that door."

Clive turned back to the shed. "W-W-What's in there?"

"Remember how I told you there are different kinds of sicknesses? Behind that door is your proof."

Clive slowly opened the door and was instantly frozen with fear. Staring back at him was one of those creatures, the very same beast that had attacked him on the train. Towering over him stood a hairy, vicious, wolf-like monster, frothing at the mouth and baring its razor-sharp teeth. The growls it let out were some of the most disturbing sounds Clive had ever heard.

Littered across the shed floor were the carcasses of countless chickens. The stench of death was enough to make even the most rugged cowboy gag.

"Werewolf," Clive whispered to himself, remembering the name of the creature from the book he had read the day before.

Just as the word left his lips, the wolf lunged. Clive squeezed his eyes shut and braced for the worst, but nothing happened. The beast had stopped short, barred from tearing him apart like it had the chickens. Its fur was matted with blood, most likely from poultry that had met their unexpected end.

Clive, trembling, turned to the old man, "You told me monsters weren't real."

"They're not," Paul said flatly. "That's my Susan."

Chapter 5

Winter Isn't as Bad as This

"Come on, Pauly, we should get a move on before it gets dark," Susan said, knowing she was the only one on this earth allowed to call Paul by that nickname.

A joking Paul replied, "Alright, alright, don't get a bee in your bonnet."

Paul loaded the last of his luggage onto the carriage and hit the trail heading west. The elderly couple, Paul at sixty-eight and Susan just a year younger, were setting out after one of the most brutal winters they could remember. Paul had heard of a small town in need of a doctor from a patient who was passing through. He could recall it vividly; it wasn't every day a grown man came in convinced he was going to die from a garter snake bite. Susan looked back one last time at their home and sighed, "I'm going to miss this place."

"Well, honey, that's alright. But we both know if we have to deal with one more snowstorm, you'll be burying me out back with our old dog Charley."

"Paul Kelp! Must you always be so morbid?" Susan scolded, covering the ears of Buck, their six-year-old bloodhound.

"Just saying it how it is, my dear," Paul said with a grin.

They were leaving behind nearly forty years of memories in that house. They had first met when a young Susan came into a just-starting-out Paul's office in hysterics after her horse had thrown her and sprained her arm. The rest was history. They were hitched six months later, it would have been sooner, but Susan didn't think a sling was a proper accessory for a wedding dress. Forty years of laughs, tears, and love had filled that house, but they both knew that as long as they had each other, it didn't matter where they ended up. They had never gotten around to having children. Paul was too busy with his practice, and it simply wasn't in the cards for the two of them.

The couple, along with Buck, rode for about three days, stopping only when the darkness made it impossible to see ahead. At night, they lay by the fire, gazing up at the stars that crowded the sky.

"I'd say by sundown tomorrow we should arrive in town. The man called it Moonlight Valley," Paul said.

"I'm just ready to sleep in an actual bed," Susan replied.

"Mrs. Kelp, are we going soft? I remember the feisty young woman who threatened to wallop a grown man for accusing me of being a snake-oil salesman."

"Yeah, well, that was thirty years and countless hair-color shades ago."

"Pish-posh, you're just as beautiful as the day we met."

"And you, Paul Kelp, are the same old sweet talker you were forty years ago. Either that, or you need to see an optometrist when we get into town," Susan chuckled. "Hey, Pauly, do you have any regrets?"

Paul turned his head from the sky to Susan and asked, "What do you mean by regrets?"

"I don't know. I think what I'm trying to say is, do you ever regret not having kids?"

"Susan, if this is your way of asking for a baby, then I hate to be the one to break the news to you, but I believe that ship has sailed. Besides, we'd need someone to change all three of us if that were the case."

Susan laughed so hard she snorted, "Not now, you goof."

"Forty years and I still know how to tickle that funny bone of yours. But in all honesty, do I ever wonder what life would have been like? Yes. I don't know a single person who goes through life without at least wondering. A little piece of you and me running around in the world." Susan turned her head from the sky, locking eyes with Paul as he continued, "But that's all it ever was, a wonder, not a regret. To say I regret not having one is to say I regret the last forty years with my best friend. And I could never regret that. So no, I never once regretted not having a child, Susan."

Susan couldn't help but smile from ear to ear. Wrapping her arm around Paul's, and with a quiver in her voice, she whispered, "Oh, Pauly, you old fool, I love you."

"I love you too. Now let's get some sleep, darlin'. We have our new palace awaiting us tomorrow."

The two fell asleep and woke just after sunrise. After another five hours of riding, they reached the town of Moonlight Valley.

"I oughta run into the jail and introduce myself to the sheriff," Paul suggested. "Shouldn't take long, and afterward we can grab a bite to eat at the saloon and get settled in at home. Keep an eye on Buck and make sure he doesn't run off, you know how excited he gets in new surroundings."

Paul walked into the sheriff's office and shook his hand, "Sheriff, I heard you were in need of a new doctor. Paul Kelp's the name."

"Sheriff Freeman. And well, Dr. Kelp, you're in luck! Our last doctor resigned a couple of weeks ago due to personal problems," the sheriff said.

Paul tilted his head like Buck when he didn't understand a command. "Personal problems?"

"Let's just say he spent more time in the saloon getting liquored up than in his office. It got so bad that I had to step in and tell him either he quits drinking, or he quits the job. So, the job's all yours, as long as you don't suffer from the same problem."

"No, sir. You don't live as long as I have by drinking yourself into a coma."

"Good. Follow me and I'll show you your new office."

Paul followed Sheriff Freeman, passing the carriage that held Susan and Buck. On the way, he gave Susan an approving wink. She sat quietly, observing the town. At first glance, she thought it was a quaint, quiet place, but certain things threw her for a loop. She couldn't quite understand why the town was split in half by train tracks. She chalked it up to a difference in design and planning.

What really stood out to her, though, were the boards nailed across the windows and doors of some houses. It left her puzzled, but she quickly wrote it off.

After Paul checked out his new office with the sheriff, he met back up with Susan at the carriage. "The sheriff said I could start tomorrow morning. For now, who's hungry?"

Susan smiled. "Famished," she replied.

The two went across the tracks and ordered a couple of steaks at the saloon, keeping Buck tied to a post outside. They toasted to their new start and hit the trail just before sundown. They had about two miles to ride outside of town before reaching their new home. Upon arriving, they released the horses from the carriage and hitched them out front.

"Just bring in what we need tonight, and I'll get the rest tomorrow. I'm beat and need a good night's sleep before my first day," he told her.

Susan agreed and carried in the necessities, such as pillows and blankets, since there was already a cot inside waiting for them. The elderly couple turned in for the night. However, Susan was soon awakened by Buck barking and growling at the front door. She tried her best to ignore it, even drifting back to sleep a couple of times, but was roused again by the persistent barking.

"Pauly? Honey? Wake up. Buck's barking at something outside."

"It's probably just an animal," Paul mumbled, half-asleep.

"I know, but the barking is keeping me up. Can you please check it out?" She shook him a few times. "Pauly, please."

Paul got up and agreed to take a look. Groggy, he grabbed his rifle and a lantern, then headed outside. Buck was still barking at the door, but Paul decided to keep him inside. He didn't want the dog running off into the night. He walked around in the brisk April air with his rifle drawn, but found nothing. When he returned to their bedroom, he looked at Susan and said, "Ain't nothin' outside."

"Really?"

"Yes, really. Now get some sleep, darlin'."

The two slept for a while longer until Susan was once again awakened by Buck's barking. She tried her best to ignore it, but couldn't, "Pauly, the dog is barking again."

Without opening his eyes, Paul said, "I just checked. There's nothing out there."

"But, Pauly—"

"No buts. I just walked around the whole house and found nothing. I've got a very important first day of work tomorrow. Now, goodnight," Paul snapped.

"Well, if you're not going to check it out, then I will."

"Okay, but I'm telling you you're just wasting your time."

Susan got out of bed and lit a lantern. She went to the front door, where Buck was going wild, and opened it. The dog bolted into the darkness. "Shoot," she muttered. She followed him into the pitch-black, able to see less than a foot ahead. "Buck... Buck," she whispered, trying not to alert any wildlife.

From the dark abyss came a disturbing yelp, followed by an even more disturbing silence. *TURN BACK!* a voice screamed inside her head, but against her better judgment, she pressed on.

She walked deeper into the night but froze when she spotted the collar of her cherished companion on the ground in front of her. Susan continued on, hoping she was getting closer to finding Buck. That is, until her eyes caught sight of a pair of claws dimly illuminated by her lantern.

Susan's eyes slowly panned up the body of the beast. There it stood, towering over the elderly woman, who was no taller than five-foot-six. Poor Buck lay motionless beside the monster. Its primal gaze met Susan's as it flashed its razor-sharp teeth, stained red from all of its previous prey. A million scenarios, all ending the same way, flashed through

Susan's head, but all the beast was focused on was the one thing it was cursed to do—hunt.

Should I run? she thought, frozen in fear. Before she had time to give it a second thought, the wolf-like monster tilted its head back toward the sky, let out a deafening howl... and made its move.

The massive creature roared and lunged at her. A bone-chilling scream tore through the night. Awoken by the sound of his wife's bloodcurdling scream, Paul turned to his left and noticed that the spot in his bed where she normally lay was empty. "Susan!" he yelled, but there was no answer. Paul pulled on his shoes, lit a spare lamp, and hurried outside. Into the night he went, shouting his wife's name.

He stumbled along for a while until he tripped over something, twisting his ankle. "Shit!" he cried, pausing to assess the damage. He shone his lantern toward the ground, and the seriousness of the situation hit him. It was the corpse of Buck. Whatever grogginess lingered instantly vanished. He wished he were still asleep, trapped in a nightmare, but deep down he knew what he was about to face was far worse.

Paul managed to get back on his feet, barely able to put weight on his right ankle. He knew it wasn't broken, he could still move it. He followed the trail of blood, which grew heavier the farther he went, until at last he found what he was dreading: Susan's body lying ahead.

"Susan!" he screamed, his voice cracking with grief, but she didn't move. Unprepared for what he was about to see, Paul limped as quickly as he could toward his wife's body.

Chapter 6

A Miracle or a Curse

"Susan! Susan! Oh my!" Paul struggled to get the words out. Susan lay motionless, unconscious, with a fatal wound to her neck. Howls and growls echoed in the distance. Paul knew he needed to get to safety. He mustered all the strength he had, lifted Susan into his arms, and tried to limp back to the house, clutching the lamp by its handle with his fingers.

The howls grew louder, signaling that the beast was closing in. He glanced back, his wife in his arms, and saw glowing eyes moving closer. Paul pushed forward as fast as he could on his injured ankle but stumbled, dropping Susan. The snarls were almost upon him. Desperate, he ditched the lamp, knowing it was a straight shot back to the house. He hoisted Susan up again and rushed forward. He could swear he felt the beast's breath on his neck as he let out a scream and slammed the door behind them.

Inside, Paul carried Susan into their bedroom and laid her on the bed. He kept repeating, "You're okay, you're okay," though he knew she was not. He lit a few candles, since the kerosene lamps were lost outside, and the risk of retrieving them wasn't worth it. Fighting back tears, Paul grabbed towels and set to work with what little medical equipment he had. First, he tried to stop the bleeding, but when that failed, he attempted CPR. His heart sank as the truth began to set in. "Close the wound, that's what I need to do," he muttered to himself.

He searched the house for his medical bag by candlelight before remembering that he had told Susan to bring in only what they needed for the night. "Shit," he said, holding his head in distress.

Paul faced two options: either accept that his wife was gone or try to limp his way to the carriage to retrieve his medical bag. He had no real idea what lurked outside. To him, it might have been a rabid animal or a pack of them.

Paul grabbed a candle and hobbled toward the carriage. He made sure not to drag his feet and kept his breathing shallow, doing everything he could to avoid drawing the attention of whatever prowled in the darkness. He frantically rummaged through their belongings until his hand closed around the medical bag. "Yes," he whispered, though he could feel eyes on him, watching like a predator stalking its prey.

Clutching the bag in one hand and the candle in the other, he stumbled back into the house. As he shut the front door behind him, he called out, "Hang in there, honey, I'm coming."

Back in their bedroom, Susan remained motionless, the blankets and sheets beneath her soaked in blood. Paul sat beside her and began cleaning and sewing the wound in her neck, speaking to her the whole time as if she could still hear him. "Hey, remember how the saloon back home always had our favorite dishes ready at the same time every night, like clockwork?"

He continued to pull fur from her wound, wiping away the saliva. Then he sterilized the wound by dampening a cloth with vinegar and pressing it against her neck for a few moments. Now that the area was prepared for surgery, Paul reached into his bag and pulled out a small container of needles and horsehair. It was time to close the gaping claw and bite marks in her neck.

"Do you remember the dish they always had ready for you?" Susan continued to lie there.

"Yeah, you remember. You'd order that beef chili with pinto beans and a side of cornbread. And to drink, you'd wash it down with a cup of piping hot coffee. It didn't matter what time of day it was, you always had to have a cup of coffee. I'd tease you about it, ask if you weren't worried it would keep you up all night. And you'd just smile and say,

'I'll have plenty of time to sleep when they put me in the ground,'" Paul's voice cracked as he spoke, fighting back tears.

Paul finished stitching Susan's wounds and lay down beside his wife in his usual spot, wishing someone would wake him from this nightmare. He knew this was the last night he would ever lie next to his wife of forty years. Feeling exhaustion sink in, he kissed her cheek and whispered, "Goodnight, sweetie," for the final time.

Paul was awakened the next morning by the unsettling sound of his wife's screaming. Not fully awake, he turned to his left where her lifeless body had been, only to see her standing over the bed, covered in blood, her face twisted in terror. "Paul, are you okay? Where did all this blood come from?" she cried.

Paul sat up and stared at her in disbelief. "Susan..." he whispered, "is that you?"

The stench of iron permeated the room.

"Of course it's me, you old fool! What happened to you, and why are we covered in blood?"

Paul bolted upright, wincing in pain, unable to tear his eyes from her. "Susan, you don't remember anything from last night?"

"What do you mean? I remember going to bed, but I couldn't sleep because Buck kept barking. So, I got up to check on him. Then... I remember waking up covered in blood," Susan said, her voice trembling as she stared at him in shock.

"Susan, last night you and Buck were attacked by something outside."

"What?"

"Yes. I was sleeping, but I woke up when I heard you scream. When I ran outside, you were bleeding badly from the neck."

"Paul, you're scaring me," she pleaded.

"No, you were lying there motionless. I had to pick you up and carry you back inside. I even twisted my ankle. You were... dead."

"Paul Kelp, you stop right now! I don't know what happened last night, but there's no reason for you to say such things."

He leaned closer to the right side of her neck, searching for the wound he had tried to save her from, but there was nothing. What should have been a moment of relief instead left him in disbelief.

"But if your neck is fine, then..." Paul rushed to the kitchen window and looked outside. There, still lying motionless, was the family dog, Buck. "I don't understand. If she's fine, then—" He couldn't even finish the thought before Susan let out a scream at the horrific sight beyond the glass.

"Poor Buck," she cried. "What happened?"

"That's what I've been trying to tell you. You were both attacked last night by a wild animal."

Susan grabbed Paul and screamed, "STOP! STOP! STOP!"

The two stood frozen in front of the window for a long moment before they finally began to come to terms with what had happened to their beloved pet. "Say, Susan, if you don't mind me asking... how are you feeling?"

"Besides finding out that my dog was mauled to death by coyotes, and my husband telling me I suffered the same fate, I feel fine."

"But what actually happened last night, Pauly?" Susan pleaded.

Not wanting to frighten her further, Paul decided to lie. It wasn't a story that would hold up under close scrutiny, but given Susan's hysterics, the explanation would likely suffice.

"You see, you told me Buck was making a commotion, but you couldn't tell why since it was so dark outside. After you came back to bed, I went out to see what the problem was. I opened the door, thinking he just needed to do his business, but he took off into the dark. I heard him struggle and growl, but by the time I got to him, it was too late. I could barely make out a pack of coyotes running off, and Buck was lying there bleeding. I tried to move him back into the house, but I was afraid the coyotes were still near. I ran back as fast as I could, but my old body failed me, and I fell, twisting my ankle. I limped the rest of the way and shut the door behind me before anything else could attack. I didn't want to wake you so late and upset you, so I let you sleep."

"But what about the blood? And why did you think I died?"

"I must have been so distraught by the whole ordeal that I didn't realize how much blood was on me. As for what happened with you… it must have been a nightmare, one of those disturbingly real nightmares," Paul said, fighting back tears.

Susan pulled Paul into a hug and said, "Oh, Pauly, I'm sorry. Why don't you get ready for your first day of work, and I'll try to get the blood out of the blankets. It looks like it's going to be a nice, warm day, so I'll be able to hang a clothesline outside and hopefully have them dry before you get home." Paul tried his best to put on a brave front and got ready for work. He even began to question whether the events of the previous night had been real or if they had unfolded the way he described them to his wife.

"What about Buck?" Susan asked.

"What do you mean?"

"Well, would you like me to bury him, or should I wait until you get home?"

Paul stood there, uncertain of what to say. He limped into the bedroom, grabbed the bloody comforter from the bed, and dragged it outside. He walked over to the deceased dog, covered it with the blanket, and limped back toward the house.

"There," he said quietly. "I'll bury him tonight after I get home, once the sun sets and it's not so hot outside."

Paul went into the bedroom and removed his blood-soaked clothes, quietly whimpering so Susan wouldn't hear and grow upset. He dressed for the day and walked out to the kitchen, where Susan was waiting.

"Pauly, I went out to the well and filled a bucket of water so you and I can wash up before you go into town. Don't want anyone thinking you massacred someone," she said with a faint smile.

"Thanks, sweetie. Do you know if we packed my cane?"

"What cane?"

"Remember the cane with the brass head? I needed it after my horse got spooked, bucked me off, and I broke my leg, years ago."

Susan thought for a moment. "If we did pack it, it would be on the carriage with the rest of the things we didn't bring in last night."

Paul made his way outside to the carriage, searching through everything they had brought with them on their journey west. He rummaged through the mess he had made the night before and finally found the cane buried at the bottom. Paul hobbled back toward the house and, forcing a grin, called out, "Found it!" Susan was at the table, wiping her face and hands with a washcloth.

"Oh, I'm glad, honey. Don't worry, before you get home, I'll bring the rest of the things in from the carriage," she replied.

"Thank you, dear. Now, if you don't mind handing me that washcloth, I need to finish cleaning up before I head out to the office."

"Okay. While you do that, I'll go saddle your horse for you," Susan suggested.

"Are you sure?"

"Do you really think I'm going to let my injured husband, who only ended up that way because I was such a nag last night, strain himself and risk getting hurt even worse? You sure you didn't hit your head last night, too?"

"Okay, thank you, Susan," he said with a chuckle.

Paul finished washing up and walked outside to Susan, who had already gotten his horse ready. He kissed her on the forehead and then, with a slight struggle, mounted the horse. He gave her a small half-wave before riding off.

The whole way to Moonlight Valley, he replayed the events of last night over and over in his head. *Was it just a nightmare?* he wondered. *It felt so real... and what about all the blood?* Paul couldn't explain what had happened. But he was a man of science and refused to believe in miracles or in anything that couldn't be explained.

Paul arrived in Moonlight Valley, and before long, he had his first patient. It was a young man, about twenty-four, who introduced himself as Ricky Clayborn. The man looked to be in good health and showed no visible signs of illness.

"What appears to be the problem?" Paul asked.

"Well, Doc, I feel great. It's just... I wake up, and I don't know how to explain it. I wake up in a random place with no recollection of how I got there."

"What do you mean?"

"I mean, almost every night I'll fall asleep and then wake up in different parts of my house or even completely random places outside. For example, this morning I woke up behind my house by the woodshed, with my clothes completely ripped."

"Do you have any new stressors in your life? A new job, perhaps, or anything unusual?"

"Not that I can recall. Why?"

"Well, usually stress can lead to sleepwalking."

"Sleepwalking?"

"That's right. More folks suffer from it than you might think, but they keep it secret out of fear that people will think they're crazy. Unfortunately, you just said stress isn't a big factor in your life. Are you a heavy drinker, Mr. Clayborn?"

"I do enjoy a nice mug of beer at the end of a long day. Why?"

"Does one glass turn into two, then three, and so on?"

"I mean, occasionally. But I don't see how that has anything to do with me waking up in different places and not remembering the night before," the young man said, his tone carrying a slight edge of defiance.

Paul looked him in the eye and said, "I'm not here to tell you how to live your life. You came to me for a diagnosis about why you keep waking up in different places, and my prognosis is this: lay off the alcohol, Mr. Clayborn. I know it may seem like a long time ago, but I was once young myself and enjoyed partying at the local saloon. Trust me, if you cut back on the beer, you'll notice a drastic difference in where you wake up, and you'll save money on getting your clothes sewn up."

"I hope you're right, Doc," Ricky said, his tone edged with offense.

The rest of the day was rather uneventful for Paul. He treated a few patients for heat exhaustion and another young woman for the same issue Mr. Clayborn had come in with. He found it odd, but diagnosed her case as stress, since her husband was away on business back east. Although unusual, he didn't dwell on it once all the facts were presented. After all, he was a man of science.

A little after five o'clock, it was closing time for the new doctor. After locking the door, Paul was stopped on his way to his horse.

"Was the first day a success, Doc?" a voice called from behind him.

Paul turned around and noticed it was the sheriff. "Hello, Sheriff. Yes, everything went rather well today, although a few cases were quite peculiar."

"What do you mean?"

"Well, first, there was a young man, Ricky Clayborn, who kept waking up in different places with ripped clothing.

We eventually determined it was likely from having a few too many drinks, which led to sleepwalking. Then there was a young woman who came in with a very similar problem, but we concluded it was stress from her husband being away."

"That is pretty odd, but nothing that should raise any concern. We've had problems with Mr. Clayborn having one too many, and you're probably right about the young woman sleepwalking."

"Yeah, it's just odd how similar the cases were."

"Well, every town has its fair share of characters. You mean to tell me that back where you're from, they didn't have drunks or people dealing with stress?"

"No, you're right," Paul said, looking down at his shoes. "It's been a long night, and I'm probably just overthinking it."

"Trouble at home, Doc?"

Paul looked up from his shoes. "Last night, coyotes, or some kind of wild animal, attacked and killed our dog. My wife was devastated when she woke up."

"I'm sorry to hear that, but these parts have a lot of wildlife such as coyotes and wolves. You'll need to be extra careful, especially at night. You look exhausted, so I won't keep you any longer. Make sure you get a good night's sleep because your job requires you to make split life-or-death decisions. I can't have you dead on your feet."

"You're right, Sheriff Freeman, and don't you worry. I'll be fresh as a daisy tomorrow."

Paul set off for home, trying to forget about the long day he'd just had, especially the events earlier. The ride home was peaceful, the sun was setting, and there was a slight cool breeze on his face. That peace ended when he came upon the bloody blanket where Buck still lay beneath it. He hitched his horse and headed inside.

"What smells so good?" he asked, medical bag in hand.

"Nothing special, just rabbit stew," Susan replied.

With a kiss on her cheek, he told her, "You know I love rabbit stew."

"I know. Do you think I'd make something you don't like, you old fool? Now sit down before it gets cold."

The two sat down and ate dinner, talking about their day. Paul told her about a few cases that came in, and Susan shared her day of cleaning up around the new house. She was proud that she had managed to get most of the bloodstains out of the sheets.

As they finished, Susan started clearing the table while Paul went outside to fetch water for the dishes. By this time, the sun had fully set, and he needed a kerosene lamp to see.

He brought the water back, and as Susan began washing the dishes, she said, "I'll finish these if you can go out and start digging the hole for Buck."

"Of course," Paul said, not wanting to say goodbye to his cherished pet.

With the help of his cane and a lamp, he made his way to the tool shed and grabbed a shovel. He walked over to the dog, whispered, "I'm sorry," and began digging Buck's final resting place.

As Paul dug about two feet down, he suddenly heard the crash of plates from inside the house.

"Susan!" he yelled, hurrying back with the lamp in one hand and the shovel in the other. His eyes were not prepared for what they were about to see.

On the kitchen floor, writhing in pain and foaming at the mouth, was Susan. Paul stood over her, trying everything he could to calm her down, but nothing worked. Her limbs began to stretch, her face twisting into a grotesque distortion. Her clothes, along with her skin, tore, replaced by coarse hair and claws. Her eyes turned a sickly yellow, and her teeth sharpened as her screams warped into a deep, guttural roar.

Paul shouted in terror as the monster began to tower over him. The beast lunged at the old man, and he collapsed in sheer fear. He crawled under the kitchen table, but within moments the table was sent flying aside by the monster with a blood-curdling howl.

"Susan, it's me, Paul!" he cried, trying desperately to reason with the beast.

Paul backed into the corner of the kitchen, torn between fighting and accepting his grim fate. The monster stalked him slowly, then grabbed his leg, dragging him closer and closer. Its paw-like hand clamped over his mouth, muffling his screams.

Paul thrashed wildly, arms stretching out for something, anything that might save him. The creature leaned in, nose to nose with him, flashing its fangs before tilting back its head and unleashing a mighty howl, "AWOOO!"

At that moment, Paul's desperate hands found the shovel lying on the floor. He swung it with every ounce of strength he had, smashing it into the monster's face. *CRACK!* A sharp yelp followed, and the beast collapsed, knocked out cold.

Paul stared in disbelief at what had just happened, but he knew he didn't have much time. He scrambled to his medical bag, fumbling for a vial of laudanum, a powerful sedative. Against his better judgment, he pried open the beast's mouth and poured the liquid down its throat.

"I can't just leave it here," he told himself.

It took him a moment to settle on a solution before limping outside to Buck. He pulled the bloodstained blanket off the dog and made his way back to the house, knowing he couldn't possibly drag the massive beast with his bare hands. Paul spread the blanket out beside it, rolled the upper body onto the cloth, then the lower half. With every pull, his ankle throbbed in excruciating pain, but he managed to drag the creature outside.

After pacing and fretting over where to put her, he finally devised a plan. He went into the tool shed and found a metal pipe. Driving it into the dry earth as far as it would go, he tied one end of a spare chain to it. Without hesitation, he hauled the blanket and the beast over to the shed, looped the other end of the chain around its neck, and shut the door. Paul collapsed in front of the shed, weeping uncontrollably for nearly an hour. How could his wife of forty years have turned into a monster?

At last, he forced himself upright and limped back to the shallow two-foot hole he had begun digging earlier. Snatching up his cane, he staggered into the house, collapsed onto the bed, and sank into exhaustion, praying that by morning he would wake to find his wife beside him, laughing at his fears and telling him it had all been just a dream.

But through the long hours of the night, he woke again and again in a panic. Each time, his heart shattered as he turned to the empty space beside him and found that his wife wasn't there.

As the sun began to rise, Paul woke from his fitful sleep, alone in his bed. Fighting back tears, he grabbed his cane and made his way to the kitchen, hoping to see Susan making breakfast, only to be met with silence and the kitchen table still lying overturned.

Teary-eyed, Paul stepped outside, passing Buck, who was now covered in flies, before limping toward the tool shed.

He knocked on the shed door. "Susan… you in there?" he asked, struggling to force the words out.

"Paul? Is that you?" came a weak, confused voice.

With a deep breath, he opened the door to reveal Susan shaking with fear.

"W-W-What happened to me? Why is there a chain around my neck?" she asked, her fragile, elderly fingers caressing the cold steel around her neck.

Paul just stood there, staring at her in silence.

"Paul Kelp, what happened? Why did you do this to me? Answer me!"

"You attacked me last night! I had no choice."

"What do you mean I attacked you?"

"I know you're not going to believe me, but… you turned into a monster."

"A what? Paul, we've played jokes on each other in the past, but don't you think this is going way too far?"

"You don't understand," he said. "You were a monster, a wolf-like creature with razor-sharp teeth and claws."

"Paul Kelp, the joke is over. You let me out this instant."

"I can't," he whispered. "For my safety and everyone else's, I just can't."

He kissed his wife on the forehead and told her he loved her before walking out and closing the door behind him as Susan screamed. With tears in his eyes, Paul returned to the house, got ready for the day, and headed to work so none of the townsfolk would suspect anything. Before going to his office, he stopped by the general store and purchased a lock for the tool shed door.

Paul spent the rest of the day working at his office, the night's events replaying in his mind again and again. Today was much busier than yesterday, with a line of patients already waiting outside before he even opened. By the time he examined the third patient, he knew something wasn't right with this town. Two people suffering from sleepwalking and memory loss was one thing, but half the town? That was different. Something was wrong.

Not feeling right about the whole situation, Paul made his way to the sheriff's office after closing. "Good afternoon, Doctor Kelp," Sheriff Freeman greeted him as he walked through the door.

"Good afternoon, Sheriff. Do you have a minute?"

"What can I do for you?" the sheriff asked with a smile, settling into his chair.

Paul, his face etched with concern, looked at the sheriff and said, "I'm worried about the folks in this town."

"Why's that?" the sheriff asked. "It seems an unusually large number of people are suffering from memory loss and waking up in strange places."

"Not this again."

"But Sheriff, yesterday I could chalk it up to a coincidence since it was only two people. Today, however, more than half of my patients showed the same symptoms."

Sheriff Freeman sat back in his chair and folded his hands. "Well, Doc, I don't know what to tell you. If you panic over a few people who can't sleep, what are you gonna do when someone gets shot? People's lives are in your hands, and I need someone steady, not someone who screams there's a public health scare because folks can't rest at night.

Now, if that's going to be a problem, you'd better tell me now."

Paul stared at him, biting his bottom lip. "No, sir," he replied.

"Good. Now, if you don't mind closing the door behind you, I'm a very busy man."

Fuming, Paul stormed out of the office, mounted his horse, and headed home. The ride was filled with muttered curses aimed at the sheriff and his dismissive attitude toward the townsfolk's suffering. When he finally rode up to the house at sunset, he let out a heavy sigh, unaware of what awaited him.

Inside, he heated up the leftover stew from the night before and poured a glass of water. With both in hand, he walked over to the shed and opened the door. Susan sat with her back to him, staring blankly at the wall.

"Susan, honey, are you hungry?"

She didn't reply or turn around. Paul, knowing how upset she was with him, said, "I'm sorry. I promise I'll fix this," as he set the food on the ground and shut the door behind him. Paul went inside, and while he was eating dinner, he heard a sudden scream from the shed. He lit a lamp, grabbed his cane, and hurried outside. When he opened the shed door and raised the lamp, it revealed the wolf-like monster that had attacked him the night before.

He froze, studying it as it stared back at him, growling viciously. Before it had a chance to lunge, he slammed the shed door shut and looked around in desperation.

Paul walked over to Buck and dragged his body to the shed. With trembling hands, he pushed the dog's body past the threshold as a sort of peace offering. The wolf seized the carcass and began to devour it, the disturbing sounds of its feeding filling the night.

Paul quickly shut the door and pulled the lock from his pocket, securing it to ensure the beast couldn't escape. Standing there, listening to the grotesque feeding inside, he placed a hand against the shed door and swore to himself once more that he would find a way to fix this.

Chapter 7

Beauty Is Now the Beast

The rabid monster lunged at Clive, its claws swiping as it tried to maul him. Clive closed his eyes, accepting his fate, but after a moment, he realized he was still standing. He looked down at his hands, making sure that was truly the case.

The monster's attack had been stopped by the chain locked around its throat, fastened to a metal pipe driven into the ground. Now only inches from his face, it let out violent growls while baring its teeth.

"Is that the beast from the train?"

"What?"

Clive turned to the elderly man and repeated, "The monster. That's the same one from the train, the one that attacked me."

"Are you deaf? I just told you that it was my Susan," Paul replied, his gun still trained on him.

"No, that can't be true. You mean to tell me there's more than one of those creatures out there?"

Clive turned back to the monster, studying it. He knew he had shot the beast back on the train, but this one showed no sign of injury, at least none he could see beneath the thick fur and streaks of chicken blood covering it. Paul poked Clive's lower back with the rifle again. "Pick up the lantern. I have something to show you," Paul said.

Clive didn't move, still in shock from what he was witnessing. He took a second to weigh his options. He could run into the blackening night, but the old man would definitely shoot him before he got far. Not to mention that the monster he was staring at was proof that there were more on the loose. The other option was to try and wrestle the gun away from Paul, but he would certainly be dead before he finished the attempt.

The old man yelled, "Hey! I said pick up the lantern and let's go."

"Okay, okay, take it easy," Clive responded while picking up the lantern.

"Good. Now walk toward the house slowly, and don't get any ideas because you'll be dead before you can blink."

Clive led the way slowly, dragging his feet with the muzzle of the rifle pressed firmly into his back. He couldn't tell if the heavy sweating was from the blistering heat of the July night or from the fact that his life was on the line. Paul pressed the gun into his back even harder, signaling for him to pick up the pace. Through the door they walked, Paul locking it behind them.

"Back of the house," he instructed Clive.

Clive walked through the kitchen and down the hall as instructed. They approached the locked door in the back of the house, where Paul had claimed a sick Susan was behind. If Susan wasn't behind the door, then what was?

Paul opened the door to reveal a bedroom littered with pages of diagrams and open books. Clive walked in, shocked by what was in front of him. The diagrams resembled what he had seen in the book a day earlier, illustrations of the monstrous werewolf. He walked over to an open book that described details about the creature, its average height, weight, and diet.

"What is all this?" Clive asked.

Lowering his gun, Paul replied, "This is my bedroom and also my study. You see, Clive, I have spent months trying to figure out how my wife was turned into one of these monsters. Some of the literature refers to them as werewolves, and others refer to them as lycanthropes. Some also say they only turn when there is a full moon, but that's a bunch of bull, because my poor Susan has turned every night since she was attacked. You know what I call them? A damn atrocity against nature, something you'd only hear about in these books or around campfire tales."

"Why did you make me believe I was going crazy about what I saw on the train that night?"

"You can't go town to town telling people you saw a human turn into a giant wolf. You cross a man who's having an off day, and he'll put a bullet in you just for insulting his intelligence. Not to mention the shitstorm the world would be in if one of those were on the loose riding a train, like you described."

"Okay, but you're not just any man, Paul. Your wife is one of those creatures. So why lie to me?"

Paul began to pace with a slight limp. "You just don't know how to follow instructions, do you? I welcomed you into my home and told you not to snoop around. Now look what happened."

"That's right, look at all of this. We know how to kill these damned monsters."

Paul stopped pacing and stared at Clive. "Kill them? What in the world are you talking about? I'm going to save them."

"Save them?"

"That's right, save my lovely wife and save the good people of Moonlight Valley."

Clive's jaw dropped. "You mean to tell me there's a whole town full of those monsters? How do you know that?"

"Remember I told you there are some sicknesses you can't, see? I don't know if it's the whole town or the majority of it."

"Have you seen anyone from town turn?"

"Well, no, but it's not a coincidence that so many people have no memory of anything after sundown and wake up somewhere completely random, wearing little or no clothes. You've also seen all those houses with windows and doors boarded up. Those folks are clearly trying to keep something out. That sheriff might not have the common sense to put two and two together, but I certainly do."

"Do you think the sheriff knows?" Clive asked.

"No. I think he's too oblivious to what's going on around him. I never saw a sheriff close by sundown. He's probably home doing what he does best, nothing."

"Okay, so how do we save them? There must be an explanation in these books."

Paul looked at the floor. "That's just it, nowhere in any of these does it say how. I've even ridden a hundred miles in every direction, talking to potion sellers and witch doctors, hoping for a cure."

"And?"

"Those who didn't laugh in my face told me the only way to deal with a werewolf is by shooting it with a silver bullet or destroying its body."

"Then that's what we have to do," Clive suggested.

Paul's head shot up, and he stared Clive in the eye as he raised his rifle. "We will do no such thing."

"What are you talking about? You even said yourself there's no way to save them. These things are monsters."

"Shut your mouth. That's my wife out there, and those townsfolk have no idea what they're doing. They're good people, you hear me? Now, I haven't found the solution yet, but it's out there."

Clive looked dumbfounded. "We have to kill them before more get out and infect others."

"I'm sorry you feel that way, Clive. Now grab the lamp and let's go."

Paul nudged Clive with the rifle to show he wasn't playing around. Clive picked up the lamp and led the way out of the room, through the kitchen, and outside. Paul had him lead all the way to the front of the tool shed, where the door remained open and the monster growled, straining at the chain it was attached to.

"Alright now, in you go," Paul said, pushing the barrel of the rifle into Clive's back.

"What?"

"You heard me. Drop the lamp and go into the shed."

Clive raised his hands, lantern in his right, showing he wasn't a threat, and turned to face the elderly man. "Come on, Paul, there has to be another way."

"There was another way, but you couldn't do what you were told. I was going to let you stay here and get back on your feet. You just had to be defiant. I guess I shouldn't expect anything less from a murderer. Now I can't have you going to another town and telling anyone what you saw here. They would surely come here and kill her, not to mention burn Moonlight Valley to the ground. Not a chance. Those good people don't deserve that."

"I promise I won't tell anyone. Just let me go."

"You're seriously promising that after already defying and lying to me? It's too risky."

Clive continued to plead, "If I go in there tomorrow morning, I am just going to come back to life. This solves nothing."

"Judging by what I have seen, you only turn if you are attacked and bitten with your heart and brain left intact. Once you go in there and I lock the door behind you, I can almost guarantee Susan won't leave anything even remotely resembling you."

"Paul, listen to yourself, this is not Susan, it's a monster."

"Shut up, Clive! Once the sun rises, it turns back into my beautiful wife. And even when she is like this, I've looked into the beast's eyes and can see she is still in there. I vowed to her that I would make it right. Now get in there."

"Please, Paul, no."

"Did the man you robbed and murdered plead for his life like you're doing now? If it makes you feel any better, consider it atoning for your sins. Now get in there."

"No."

Paul raised the rifle to eye level and screamed, "Get in there now, or I'll shoot you right here!"

Clive turned around and stepped closer to the feral beast. Saliva dripped from its mouth as if it knew Clive was going to be its next victim. Clive inched closer, stalling for time as he tried to come up with a way out. That's when he looked down at the kerosene lamp in his right hand. He raised it and hurled the lamp at the shed, shattering it. Flames erupted, and the shed caught fire.

The beast swatted at the growing blaze as the flames began to surround it. Paul yelled, "NO! SUSAN!" as he dropped the rifle and tried to free the werewolf before it was consumed. He yanked on the chain and tried to pull the metal pole from the ground, but it was no use. The dry weather fed the flames, and soon the entire shed was an inferno. The quiet night filled with the howls of the beast and the anguished screams of a husband desperate to save his wife.

Chapter 8

A Fox in the Hen House

"I'm sorry," Clive muttered as he watched the inferno burn. Deep down, he knew that if what Paul had said was true, he needed to warn the sheriff, who remained completely oblivious that the town had been overrun by werewolves. But he also remembered Paul's warning: nobody was ever at the jail after dark. There was no sense in risking his life with those monsters roaming outside.

Clive picked up the rifle and headed back into the house, making sure the door was shut tight behind him in case the fire and Paul's screams drew more of those vicious creatures. He went straight into Paul and Susan's room, searching for answers. Moving around the werewolf shrine, he read carefully, hoping to find something Paul had overlooked— anything that might reveal how to reverse the effects of a werewolf bite. Without that knowledge, there would be no way to destroy an entire town full of lycanthropes.

Clive worked tirelessly through the night, poring over documents and testimonials of werewolf encounters. By the time he looked up, the sun had been shining for a couple of hours. He knew it was time to make his way to Moonlight

Valley and warn the sheriff about the events of the night before, the doctor's fate, and the danger threatening the entire town.

Clive walked out of the house, exhausted, and made his way to the horse Paul had let him borrow to ride into town. As he rode away from the property, he passed the shed, now nothing more than a pile of burnt lumber and ash. Among the rubble lay the charred remains of Paul and the beast. Clive stared for a moment and whispered, "This won't be for nothing, Paul. I'll stop this."

He continued toward Moonlight Valley, trying to figure out how he could tell the sheriff about the werewolves overrunning the town without sounding like a lunatic.

When he arrived, Clive headed straight for the jail. It was still early, so he hitched his horse and waited by the door for the sheriff to arrive. About an hour later, he spotted a figure riding in on horseback, wearing a ten-gallon hat. Clive knew immediately this was the man he had been waiting for. The sheriff pulled up, hopped down, and hitched his horse next to Clive's.

"Mornin', Sheriff," Clive said.

The sheriff walked right past him, the taps of his snakeskin boots echoing against the wooden deck, and went through the front door without a word. Clive frowned at the odd behavior, but instead of taking the hint that the sheriff didn't want to be bothered so early, he followed him inside. Sheriff Freeman was already at his desk, bent over paperwork. Clive cleared his throat and tried once again to get his attention.

"Um, pardon me, Sheriff, do you have a moment?"

Sheriff Freeman didn't look up, continuing to scratch away at his paperwork.

"Alright, Sheriff, I don't know how to say this, so I'm just gonna come out with it, you're all in danger!"

That got the sheriff's attention. He finally looked up at Clive and asked, "What do you mean we're all in danger?"

"Werewolves!" Clive blurted.

"Were—what?"

Knowing he was too deep to back out now, Clive met the sheriff's gaze. "Werewolves," he repeated.

"And what exactly is a werewolf, if you don't mind me asking?"

"I know this is going to sound crazy, but they're giant wolves."

"Trust me, Mr...?"

"Clive."

"You have a last name, Clive?"

"Holiday, sir."

"Mr. Clive Holiday," the sheriff said evenly, "we're all aware of the wolf and coyote problem we've got here. But trust me, folks around here know how to handle themselves. It comes with living out here."

"What? No. I don't mean the regular wolves you and I are accustomed to. I mean giant wolves—people by day, monsters by night."

The sheriff chuckled, shaking his head. "Hah! I see you've been hitting the saloon early, Mr. Holiday."

"What are you laughing at? We're all in danger! They're coming for you, me, and they even killed Paul Kelp."

"Paul Kelp? You mean Doctor Kelp? How do you know him?"

"The doctor was helping me get back on my feet after I was injured in an accident. His wife was one of those monsters, and he had her chained up in the tool shed. He was afraid I'd tell someone about his secret, so he tried to force me into the shed with her. Before I did, I lit the shed on fire, which resulted in both of them burning."

"So, what you're telling me is that you killed the doctor and his wife?"

"I'm saying his wife was a werewolf, and I was defending myself from becoming her next meal. Now I'm here to tell you that Doctor Kelp told me many of the people who live in this town have the same sickness in them."

"Alright, Mr. Holiday, I'm going to ride up to the Kelps' property and investigate, but I'm going to need you to stay right here until I get back. Do you think you can do that for me?"

"Don't you want me to show you where it is?"

"No, no. You stay. I'm well aware of where their property is, but if someone comes in looking for me, tell them I'll be right back and no talk about these wolf monsters, if you could."

"Can do," Clive exhaled, relieved that someone believed him.

Sheriff Freeman mounted his horse and rode to the Kelps' property. When he arrived, he dismounted and walked toward the still-smoldering shed. He stared for a long moment at the unrecognizable, charred remains lying before him, removing his hat and covering his nose with it to block the stench of death.

He moved on to the house. In the kitchen, the table was overturned, evidence of an immense struggle. When he stepped into the bedroom, the sheriff was taken aback by the sheer amount of research on werewolves that filled the room.

He pulled one of the diagrams from the wall, folded it neatly, and slipped it into his back pocket.

Freeman then rode back to Moonlight Valley, where Clive sat waiting anxiously for his return.

The sheriff stepped through the front door, and Clive leapt from his seat, rushing toward him. Without hesitation, Freeman drew his revolver and barked at him to stay put, warning against any sudden movements. He frisked Clive for weapons, taking his money and pocket watch in the process. Then he forced Clive into a cell, locked the door, and returned the key to the hook hanging on the wall.

"What is this all about?" Clive shouted.

"You're under arrest for the murder of Paul and Susan Kelp."

"I didn't kill anyone!"

"Well, there's a burned-down shed with two bodies so badly charred that there's no way to even identify them."

"I already told you what happened!"

"Ah, yes, the werewolves caused the fire, killing both of them."

"No! His wife was already a werewolf, and I had to burn the shed down to save my life."

"And the doctor?"

"The doctor held me at gunpoint until I started the fire. Then he ran in to free the monster, his wife, but got trapped inside."

"I see," Sheriff Freeman reached into his back pocket, pulled out a diagram of a werewolf, and held it up. "Did she happen to look like this?"

Clive's eyes widened, and he shouted, "YES! THAT'S IT! THAT'S THE MONSTER!"

The sheriff raised his hand, motioning for Clive to lower his voice. "This right here is nonsense. A creature from tall tales, like sea serpents. And you expect me to believe these things are running wild in my town? What kind of fool do you take me for, Mr. Holiday?"

"But Paul told me most of the townsfolk were suffering from memory loss and sleepwalking!" Clive insisted.

"And that's your evidence? You expect me to believe these people are turning into wild animals? It's called stress, Mr. Holiday. And judging by the exhaustion on your face and the bandage on your arm, you're no stranger to it. What's next? Am I supposed to believe you're turning into a ghost or a goblin? You'd better come up with a stronger defense, or the judge will have no trouble sentencing you to hang for your crime. Now, if you'll excuse me, I've got business in the jail's basement before the train comes through with my shipment. Damn thing passes through in the early hours of the morning, waking hard-working folks like me from a deep slumber."

Clive tried to plead his case, but it was useless, the sheriff was already out of earshot. He couldn't understand why Sheriff Freeman refused to believe him. Then again, if he hadn't lived through the nightmare himself, he wouldn't have believed it either.

Clive collapsed onto the cot in his cell, drifting in and out of uneasy sleep, waiting for someone, anyone who might listen and believe him.

Chapter 9

This Is a Witch Hunt

Clive was awakened by the sound of the train stopping in the center of town. Sheriff Freeman came up from the basement to go outside and help unload goods from the train. With the help of a few townsmen, they carried wooden crates into the jail's basement. Clive counted at least ten, maybe fifteen.

Clive asked one of the men what was in the crates as the man came back up from the basement. The burly fellow pushed up to the bars and spat in his face. "That's for Doctor Kelp," he said.

"I didn't kill him! It was a beast! Why doesn't anyone believe me?"

"Maybe it's because of the hocus-pocus explanation you gave about last night," the sheriff chimed in, thanking the men for their help. "It's close to closing time, which means I have to feed you; I'll run to the saloon and grab food and a glass of water."

"Thank you."

Sheriff Freeman stepped close to the bars, his face grave. "Don't thank me. If it were up to me, I'd let you starve for what you've done."

"But I didn't do anything," Clive pleaded once again.

The sheriff scoffed at Clive before leaving the jail. When he returned, he carried a plate of what could only be described as slop and a piece of white bread. A dirty glass of water accompanied it, looking like it had dysentery written all over it. The sheriff handed the plate to Clive, who didn't appear at all appetized by the meal.

"What's wrong? Not the fine feast you were hoping for?" Freeman asked.

Not wanting to give the sheriff the satisfaction of seeing his misery, Clive picked up the bread, dipped it into the brown slop, and said, "Looks great."

"Alright, you enjoy that. Depending on how tomorrow's trial turns out, it might be your second-to-last meal."

"I have to wait until tomorrow to plead my case and be set free?"

"The judge can't reach town until morning. Normally, you'd wait a few days here, but given the severity and the pure hatred behind this crime, he's decided justice should be dealt to the one responsible immediately."

"Will I have a jury of my peers?"

"Normally you would, but considering you killed a well-respected doctor and his wife, I gotta tell you, Mr. Holiday, you don't have any peers here. That being said, you'll have better luck with just the judge deciding whether you walk free or not. I'll leave you with this, you've got about as much chance of walking out of here as you do of seeing one of those monsters roaming the street."

The sheriff left for the night, and all Clive could do was sit there, trying to come up with a defense that wouldn't make him seem insane. Then, without explanation, his head spun and his eyelids grew heavy. Odd considering that only moments ago, he'd been filled with piss and vinegar. He tried his best to stay awake, knowing he needed every moment to formulate a coherent defense for the morning. This wasn't some petty theft Clive was on trial for; it was murder, and he knew he couldn't afford to close his eyes. He fought the fatigue as long as he could, but eventually, exhaustion claimed him.

Clive slept through the night and only stirred once when he could have sworn he heard the jail door creak open. His eyes barely fluttered, too heavy to lift, leaving him unsure whether it was real or just his half-dreaming mind. Still, he could have sworn he heard the howls of those monsters not just outside, but echoing from somewhere beneath him.

Not even sleep could grant Clive relief from the nightmare his life had become. Standing before the judge, sweat gathered at his brow as he pleaded his case. After the sheriff delivered his testimony, the judge, after only a brief pause for thought, found Clive guilty. Overcome with disbelief, Clive broke down, his desperate cries echoing through the courtroom, prompting the judge to call him forward for sentencing.

"He'll hang for sure," Clive heard the sheriff say in a jovial whisper.

As Clive stepped forward, the judge, a pudgy, pale-looking man, suddenly dropped to the ground and started to scream. Sheriff Freeman rushed forward to help as the man's body began to shake uncontrollably.

"No, no, no, this can't be happening!" Clive cried. Just as he had witnessed before, the judge's skin began peeling away, revealing the abomination underneath.

Freeman, frozen in shock, didn't know what to think. Before he could react, a claw shot up and slashed across his face. Writhing in pain, Freeman screamed and fell back, revealing a deep, jagged gash along his cheek.

The judge, now fully transformed into one of those beasts, rose to his feet and let out a mighty howl. Clive tried to run, but before he could get far, the monster leapt over the injured sheriff and crashed down on top of him, knocking him to the floor.

The werewolf stood over Clive, its breath hot and foul as it leaned in close. Staring into the creature's eyes, Clive froze. There was nothing he could do, not even scream. The monster opened its mouth, revealing razor-sharp teeth dripping with saliva. This was it for Clive, he knew he was about to meet his grim fate.

"Alright, wake up," a voice commanded, dragging Clive back from the edge of his nightmare.

Clive jerked awake, covered in a cold sweat, his body moving at half speed.

"Come on, get up. We can't keep the judge waiting all day," said Sheriff Freeman. Clive stood and found himself face-to-face with Freeman.

"Yeah, not really in a rush to hear someone tell me that by this time tomorrow, I'll be hanged in the middle of town."

"Maybe you should have thought of that before you went off the deep end and murdered the Kelps."

"I told you, I didn't do anything."

"Save it for the judge," The sheriff cuffed Clive and shoved him out the jailhouse door. He was led through the dusty street to the saloon, where the judge waited, holding Clive's future in his hands.

As Clive pushed through the swinging doors, he spotted a short, pudgy man seated behind one of the tables. His heart began to pound as the nightmare from the night before flashed vividly in his mind.

"What if he's a werewolf, like in my dream, and attacks all of us?" he thought. *"The sun's up, so that should be impossible, but what if the books were wrong? It's not like there's definitive proof these things even exist,"* his mind continued to race.

The judge remained seated as the sheriff and a cuffed Clive stood before him. "Gentlemen, I have been briefed on the case by Mr. Freeman here, but I'm here to hear both sides without prejudice. Now, let's start with you, Sheriff."

"Your Honor, I'm here to speak on behalf of Paul and Susan Kelp. They couldn't make it here today to speak for themselves because Mr. Holiday here, by his own admission, burned them both alive in a fit of insanity. It was up to me to investigate his motives, and I believe I've gathered sufficient evidence to prove his guilt," Sheriff Freeman declared.

"Alright, Mr. Freeman, you may proceed," the judge directed.

"Mr. Holiday told me that Paul found him injured and took him in, nursing him back to health. He bandaged his wounds and put food in his gut. And how did Mr. Holiday

93

repay such kindness? By locking the doctor and his poor, defenseless wife inside the tool shed before proceeding to rob the Kelps' home. This explains why the house was a disaster: the kitchen table overturned, chairs broken, and their belongings scattered. Angry that he couldn't find much profit to steal, Mr. Holiday disposed of the only two witnesses who could tie him to the crime by burning down the shed with Mr. and Mrs. Kelp inside. Then, trying to get ahead of the law and appear innocent, he came to the jail to report the very crime he had committed. Lacking a concrete alibi, he blamed everything on a mythical creature he claims to have read about in several books found at the Kelp residence."

The judge seemed both horrified by the crime, yet unimpressed by the explanation of a wolf-like human committing it.

"Alright, Mr. Holiday, how do you recall the events as they took place?" the judge asked.

"Well, Judge, I'll tell you, but I'm going to warn you first that what I'm about to say may sound like something out of an old tall tale. Yes, the doctor took me in after I suffered an injury, but I didn't kill him to cover up a robbery," Clive began pleading his case.

"What the sheriff said was true about the beast, but before you scoff at me, I ask you to hear me out. The doctor's wife was bitten by one of those monsters, which turned her into a werewolf every night. The doctor, afraid I might tell someone, held me at gunpoint and ordered me into the shed where he kept his wife, to prevent her from attacking him or anyone else," Clive continued, trying to make himself sound less like a madman.

"You see, I didn't mean to hurt the doctor. He ran into the fire because he believed his wife, and anyone infected by the mark of the beast, could be cured. If you don't believe me, take a look inside their house. The doctor was obsessed with researching these creatures. He had books, diagrams, and testimonials lining the walls of his room."

"You can't seriously be buying this, Your Honor."

The judge, turning his gaze toward Clive, said, "You can't really expect me to believe that his wife turned into a wolf."

"All I'm asking is that you go to the house and look in the room," Clive pleaded.

"Judge, by even considering such an idea, you're making a mockery of the justice system. Besides, you can't go check out the house; all that's left are ashes and scorched lumber."

Clive, now shouting, said, "I NEVER BURNED DOWN THE HOUSE!"

"After not finding anything he deemed valuable, Mr. Holiday set the house ablaze," Sheriff Freeman declared.

"Mr. Holiday, if you have no evidence to prove anything you're saying, then I have no choice but to find you guilty of your crimes. I hereby sentence you to death by hanging at noon tomorrow," the judge ruled.

"I didn't do what Sheriff Freeman said I did!" Clive protested.

"Please, Sheriff, take the prisoner back to his cell."

Clive was escorted out of the courtroom and back to jail. Outside, many of the residents of Moonlight Valley looked on. They may not have been inside to hear the verdict, but since Clive was still in cuffs, they knew justice, at least in their eyes, had been served.

One of the local women even yelled, "You'll burn for what you've done!"

Clive kept his head down, not wanting to provoke anyone into doing something rash. If he were being honest with himself, he wouldn't have believed any of the events he described in the courtroom if he hadn't lived through them himself.

Back at the jail, the sheriff removed Clive's cuffs and shoved him roughly into his cell.

As the day rolled on, Clive sat silently in his cell. Deep down, he knew this was a fitting end to his story. He thought back to the man he'd held up and ultimately shot dead back in Dodge City. He could make excuses all day that he hadn't meant to kill anyone, but at the end of the day, it had been his choice to rob him.

Why should he go on expecting a fresh start while an innocent man lay buried six feet under? The same went for the doctor, he had only been trying to save his wife and the people of Moonlight Valley. Clive had always known his past would catch up to him sooner or later.

He spent most of the day brooding over a way out of his predicament. His eyes kept drifting to the key hanging on the wall, the one that could set him free, allowing him to vanish into the night and leave this cursed town behind.

By this time, the sun had already begun to set, and the sheriff had presumably gone home for the night long ago. Another hour passed of Clive's final night on earth before the jail door creaked open, and to Clive's surprise, Sheriff Freeman stepped inside.

"How are you hanging in there, Mr. Holiday?" Freeman asked, mocking the grim fate awaiting Clive in the morning.

"Real funny. Hey, if the sheriff thing doesn't work out for you, and it won't, since this is a complete miscarriage of justice, you should try becoming a comedian."

"You shut your damn trap! My investigation was done with the intention of bringing justice to the Kelps, not defending the criminal who killed them."

"Well, if you were really doing your job, you would have had someone stay at the house so nobody could burn it down and destroy key evidence."

"Did it ever occur to you that the fire you started in the shed might have spread to the house? Maybe a gust of wind carried embers over and set it ablaze."

"That doesn't make any sense! You went back to the house hours after the shed burned down, and you even grabbed the werewolf diagram just to mock me. Did you ever stop to think that maybe there was foul play?"

"Foul play by who? Have you not noticed that by sundown, everyone's home, and there's not a soul left wandering the streets? That's why the saloon closes so early, it's not worth keeping open if no one's coming in. The only racket in this town after dark is the train that passes through before sunrise. Besides, I don't know why I'm the one being interrogated, especially by a murderer."

Clive, growing more furious, said, "I don't know how many times I have to say it, I didn't murder Paul and his wife!"

"You're still going with that story? Haven't you heard of innocent until proven guilty? You committed the crime, had your fair trial, and were proven guilty," Freeman said with a low chuckle.

"If you're not here to hear me out, then why are you here so late anyway?"

Sheriff Freeman smirked and slowly drew his revolver.

"What the hell are you doing pointing that thing at me?" Clive snapped, backing up.

Freeman opened the cell door and motioned for Clive to step out. The prisoner had a bad feeling about what the sheriff was planning. Was he going to lure Clive outside just to shoot him? It wasn't like anyone would call it murder. Clive was already a dead man walking.

Against his better judgment, he stepped out of the cell. The sheriff ordered him toward the back of the jail and down to the basement. Clive's nerves began to ease. If Freeman meant to kill him, he would've done it outside, no cleanup needed. But Clive had no idea what horrors awaited him below.

Chapter 10

A Wolf in Sheep's Clothing

As he reached the bottom of the basement stairs, Clive paused, letting out a deep breath. Using the barrel of his revolver, the sheriff nudged Clive forward, sending him down the last step into the darkness.

Freeman reached into his back pocket for a small book of matches and struck one against the sole of his snakeskin boot. He lit a few lamps hanging on the walls, their glow revealing a row of cramped jail cells. Inside each cell were several prisoners, some smeared with blood, others clothed in nothing more than tattered strips of fabric.

"What is this?" Clive asked, his voice unsteady.

"This is why I came back here so late," Freeman said. "Normally, I'd slip a sedative into your food like I did yesterday so I could come and go as I please, courtesy of the doctor's bag. But since you hang tomorrow, there's no harm in showing you a little 'peek behind the curtain,' if you will."

"How many people are in here?"

"I don't really know. Could be ten, maybe fifteen. Every night, it feels like I've got another person to shove into one of these cells that's why I've had to start doubling, even tripling, them up. No need to worry, though," Freeman said, pointing to the stacks of crates piled against the back wall of the basement, "because that shipment of TNT and dynamite I received the other day will let me expand down here, make room for plenty more."

"What did they do that was so terrible that you keep them down here in these conditions?"

"That's a tough one, Clive," Freeman said, his tone almost thoughtful. "See, it's not so much about what they did, it's about who they are. Most of 'em are decent folks who just happened to be in the wrong place at the wrong time. Like Mrs. Dauson over there, the poor woman was a devoted wife who happened to visit the outhouse a little too late. Or Dennis Lowery, he was out late taking a stroll to clear his head after the financial troubles that weighed him down."

"I don't understand, none of those were even crimes, let alone something so heinous that would warrant you to keep them down—" Before he could finish his thought, one of the prisoners collapsed, flailing uncontrollably across the jail floor. Moments later, a second person dropped and let out a piercing, guttural scream. Within seconds, the entire basement filled with the echoing cries of the suffering prisoners.

Their skin began to split, tearing open to reveal what lay beneath their true selves. Clive tried to turn away, but when he looked at the sheriff, he was laughing hysterically, like a man watching a stage comedy at the saloon.

After what felt like an eternity, the cells were filled with the very monsters the sheriff had so vehemently denied were real.

"T-T-Those things. You told me you didn't believe me and that I was crazy. Why didn't you tell the judge?"

Sheriff Freeman, his face still flushed from laughing, said, "Why would I go and do a thing like that? So he could make me give up my badge because he thinks I'm mad for believing in monsters? Or worse, he brings a posse back here to burn the town to the ground and kill these good folk? They didn't do anything wrong, so why should they be killed?"

"But why?"

"Simple, really. I'm sick and tired. I'm sick of spending my life with nothing. This town used to be full of people who cared for one another, but now more and more of you 'visitors' come looking for a fresh start and a way to get ahead, pushing hardworking families like ours out after a lifetime here. If those visitors want to come in and steal the jobs of us hard workers, they're never going to leave, so I decided to do something about it."

"I don't understand why you wouldn't want new people coming in, helping your town grow, and bringing in business?" Clive asked, dumbfounded and in disbelief at his own words. What Freeman was saying was the exact gripe he'd had back in Dodge City.

"Now you're starting to sound like that money-hungry Sheriff Freeman. He didn't care about the people who already lived here. He just saw dollar signs as the place grew, pushing us out. While he was busy making things better for newcomers, the folks who'd been here all along lost their jobs and had to steal just to keep their bellies full."

Clive stood there, confusion written across his face as he tried to process what he'd just heard. "But... you're Sheriff Freeman."

"Actually, that is Sheriff Freeman," the man said, pointing to one of the monsters in the cell. "Allow me to introduce myself. The name's Daniel Cody. The poor sheriff over there was attacked one night by one of those creatures on his way home from the saloon after a night of drinking. I was outside the saloon and saw him walk down an alley, then came the most vile scream I've ever heard. When I got there, he was lying in a pool of his own blood, bits of flesh hanging off of him. That's when I decided to make my move. I took his badge and his fine cowboy hat and decided to become the lawman this town truly deserves."

"Wouldn't everyone notice you weren't the real Sheriff Freeman? I mean, they must have seen him before."

Daniel smirked and let out a low chuckle. "Minor details, my friend. When the world's on fire, people turn to someone who looks like they have a plan, someone with answers. I can lead these people back to the way things were. So what if that means folks have to be home before the sun goes down and the moon rises? Not spending all night at the saloon getting drunk is a small price to pay to keep order. Besides, I've never been much of a fan of alcohol, it makes people act like wild animals," he said, finishing with a wink.

"And those who oppose?" Clive asked.

"Not everyone was on board with a former rancher assuming the identity of the town's once-beloved sheriff. Sometimes you have to make an example of those who refuse to fall in line. If that means locking someone in a cage with the sheriff, so be it. I can bring this town back to what it was, no more newcomers pushing us out of our way of life. If you were looking for a fresh start, maybe you shouldn't have blown your first chance."

"But why not just lock me in a cell with one of them? You could have brought me down here the first night without anyone knowing I existed. Instead, you went through the trouble of staging a trial and arranging a public execution."

Daniel began to pace, never taking his gun down.

"Simple, a new judge is running the circuit through these parts, and I couldn't go on forever without him putting a face to the name. So, I saw an opportune time for Sheriff Freeman to make his acquaintance. An added bonus is that it lets everyone know that if they ever try to bring outsiders back here to ruin what I've built, I will stop at nothing to make them look crazy," Daniel said, looking Clive dead in the eye. "They'll hang faster than it'll take me to put on these awfully nice boots courtesy of the good sheriff over there."

"As for the Kelps, it's a damn shame about his lovely wife. I'll admit, I was a little nervous the old man would run and tell everyone, that was until he got so caught up in a supposed cure. He wasn't going to risk anyone coming in and killing his 'monster-wife' or the people he felt responsible for here in Moonlight Valley. In the end, I didn't need to worry about any of that, did I? You came in and took out the defenseless elderly couple who would never hurt a fly. All I had to do was burn down that lousy house, tying up any loose ends. I know what you're thinking—you can't get away with this. But, Clive, once you hang tomorrow, I already have."

Clive stood there, peering from the phony sheriff to the cages filled with beasts and back. He couldn't tell whether the werewolves or Daniel was the true monster. What unsettled him most was that the madman reminded him so much of himself, an honest working man who'd fallen on hard times and turned to a life of crime. Instead of holding up poor, unsuspecting folks, he'd stolen another man's identity.

"Listen Freeman, or Daniel, you don't have to do this. You and I are more alike than you know."

Daniel scoffed at the idea of being anything like the man he'd spent the last few days setting up.

"I know you don't want to see it, but I, like you, was once a rancher pushed out by a flood of new competition. What did the town do for me, you might ask? Absolutely squat. I spent my life working my fingers to the bone, and they threw me aside like I was nothing. But murder, that makes us worse than them. We need to band together and kill these monsters. Nobody will be safe unless we do."

"Let me stop you there. Do you honestly think you're the first one to try and convince me that what's going on here is wrong? Look around, life has never been better for us. I'm not going to listen to some failed rancher who didn't have the nerve to take back his town preach to me about what's right. I reckon you have no idea of the difference between right and wrong, just as they don't. Is it right that you and your friends get pushed out of your homes because you can't afford property taxes, while the town prospers like never before? The difference between you and me is this: I'm not looking out for myself alone but for everyone here."

"You think this is looking out for your friends? You feed anyone who opposes you to those beasts behind those bars over there, and if they weren't lucky enough to be killed by them, they'd spend the rest of their lives turning into those abominations every night. Not to mention the people who don't outright object have to live in fear, knowing that just outside their houses is a feeding ground. You think you are doing this for the greater good of those who built this town, but along the way you've stepped on the necks of the very people you called friends."

Daniel's amusement disappeared, replaced by a hard edge of annoyance. "You really think, with all that research you and old man Kelp have done, that the only monsters walking around are the ones in those cells? Of course not, the sickness had to start somewhere, didn't it? The first person I locked up down here was Freeman, and after that, more and more folks began to line up outside the doctor's office, not remembering what happened the previous night or how they woke up somewhere other than their bed. I've put a curfew on the town, but people kept refusing to take it seriously and test it. As a result, that's what they turn into." He nodded toward the cages full of vicious beasts.

"It's a dog-eat-dog world out there, Clive, and I'm doing the best I can to make sure this town comes out on top."

Clive looked on in amazement.

"Do you think you're the only ones who've done research?" Daniel asked.

Clive knew there was no point in trying to talk sense into Daniel; he was a man who had been burned in the past and was now drunk on power. Part of Clive almost wished the wannabe sheriff would open the cell door and feed him to the wolves, anything to escape the dread of spending the rest of the night alone in his jail cell, thinking about his public execution tomorrow. He also knew his hanging would serve as an example for anyone who dared to speak out.

With a shove from his gun, Daniel forced Clive back upstairs to his cell, where he'd sit until his execution.

"You're going to ride back home now with those beasts roaming around out there?" Clive asked.

"How mad do you think I am?" Daniel replied with a smirk. "I'm going to spend the night right there in that chair behind my desk. Besides, I've got to be up early to make sure everything's set for your big day tomorrow. If I really need to go home, I've got a couple of insurance policies in my desk drawer."

Daniel opened the drawer and held up a single silver bullet.

"You'd be surprised how well these things work. Oh, and thanks for that silver pocket watch. It came in handy when I had the blacksmith make a few more of these beauties."

Chapter 11

Friends in Low Places

Clive woke up several times that night, unable to sleep, knowing his life would come to an end in the afternoon. Every time he woke up, he peered over at Daniel, who was asleep in his chair with his feet propped up on the desk. The bone-chilling howls from the beasts outside and downstairs were enough to keep any sane person awake in a cold sweat. He spent the rest of the night trying to come up with a plan. He thought he could rush Daniel when he opened the cell door, but in every scenario, it ended with him being shot before he could even make a grab for Daniel's gun. He continued to think until the sun started to rise and the grotesque growls from the monsters subsided. Only then did exhaustion finally overpower him, and he passed out.

"Alright! Rise and shine, today's the big day! Are you excited?" Daniel said gleefully.

Clive awoke with a groan and asked, "What time is it?"

"It's about thirty minutes until showtime. I'm surprised you'd want to spend your last moments on Earth sleeping the day away."

"Sometimes it's the only time things make sense to me."

Daniel walked over to the key hook, snatching the key off the wall. He opened the cell door and told Clive to turn around with his hands behind his back. While Daniel brought out the handcuffs, Clive thought for a brief moment of reaching for the revolver on the fake sheriff's hip. He then remembered that every outcome he had imagined last night ended with him being shot dead on the spot. Daniel cuffed him and led the prisoner outside.

Outside the jailhouse, a stage had been set up, and hanging high above it was the noose that Clive would soon occupy. It seemed like the whole town—or what was left of it—had gathered to witness Clive's execution. Some folks were silent as he was brought to the stage, while others shouted vile things at him. It turned out that Daniel had done a thorough job of brainwashing some of the people from Moonlight Valley. Daniel brought Clive to the top of the platform, and they waited for noon to arrive.

As noon drew near, the sheriff began to explain the reason for the gathering in a boisterous voice to ensure everyone could hear him.

"Ladies and gentlemen, we are gathered here today for the execution of Clive Holiday, who was found guilty of murdering Paul and Susan Kelp."

"Hang the scoundrel!" a voice from the crowd yelled.

Daniel smirked and said, "In due time, my friends. He was found guilty and sentenced to death by hanging. Now, does the prisoner have any last words before he is put to death?"

"Folks of Moonlight Valley, I know you live in fear of speaking out, but we all know this is not Sheriff Freeman. I know a lot of you feel like this town wronged you by allowing newcomers in to take your jobs and uproot your way of living. But do you really want to live in fear of leaving your home after sundown while monsters roam around outside the four walls that keep you safe? I bet most of you didn't know that the sheriff was keeping many of them in the basement of the jail. I know you all wanted change, but is living like a prisoner the way you want to exist? Afraid to go outside? Afraid of speaking up against injustice?"

The crowd fell silent as a distant look crossed Daniel's face.

"My friends, may I have a gentleman come up here and stand with the prisoner while I grab something from my office?"

A brawny man, who had to be in his mid-forties, came forward. He was dirty and had clearly taken time off work in the field to witness the occasion. His beard was slightly yellowing from age, and sweat visibly stained his white long-sleeve shirt. His outfit was complete with a cheap straw hat resting on his head. The sheriff gave him a nod of appreciation and headed towards the jail.

"Sir, please help me out of this. You know this isn't right."

The man kept staring straight ahead, but in his deep voice said, "Boy, I'd keep your mouth shut if you know what's good for you. You see those people out there? All of them are here to see you hang. You don't have a single friend out there."

The fake sheriff returned, leading a woman Clive recognized as one of the poor individuals from the cell in the basement, Mrs. Dauson. She looked absolutely defeated. The crowd was silent as she made her way to the stage. The man who had been there to ensure Clive didn't step off the stage stepped back, giving the sheriff and the woman space.

"Ladies and gentlemen, this is Mrs. Dauson. She is a loving wife. By the looks of her, she seems like she wouldn't be able to harm a fly, and you're right. When she is in this form, she would never harm anyone. You see, a few weeks ago, she took a late-night trip to the outhouse. Unfortunately, she never made it there and was mauled by one of those savage beasts in the darkness. While the attack was severe, it left her brain and heart intact. That may sound like good news to you and me; however, I am almost positive she would have preferred the beast kill her that night. Her husband found her outside the next morning, clothes torn and lying in a pool of blood. She couldn't explain the blood or why she was asleep outside, so they took her to Doctor Kelp. Later that night, she turned into one of those monsters and viciously attacked the love of her life, brutally slaying him. When she came to the next morning, she was faced with the grim reality of what she had done and came to me at the jailhouse. I investigated the crime scene and placed her in that basement where she could not hurt herself or anyone else ever again."

Daniel continued, "Now, Mr. Holiday here says we should just kill all of those creatures. Is what happened truly her fault if she had no control over herself? Not to mention, she has no memory of it at all. Everyone down in that basement has stories of being upstanding citizens of Moonlight Valley who were attacked by these monstrosities. Do you really want to kill friends and family if there is a cure out there? To prevent you from turning into one of them, all I ask is that you are inside by sundown and only come back out after sunrise. We all know the monsters I have contained down there are only a few of the many beasts that roam the streets of this town at night."

Daniel had the remaining citizens in the palm of his hand. To be honest, his argument was so compelling that if Clive didn't know any better, he might have believed it himself. The crowd had already found him guilty, so there was no reason for Clive to spend his last moments pleading for his life. The sheriff walked to the end of the stage and held up a burlap sack to the crowd. They cheered as he placed it over Clive's head, followed by the noose. Daniel had him stand at the edge of the stage and shoved him off.

On the other side of the burlap sack, Clive could hear the crowd shift from cheers of celebration to screams of fear. He kicked his feet as he dangled above the ground when, suddenly, someone in the crowd fired a shot at Daniel. The shot came from a revolver, nearly missing Daniel and hitting the middle-aged man in the chest, knocking him off the stage. As he fell off the back of the stage, the rest of the crowd fled for safety. Gunfire erupted from multiple directions, killing a couple of the bloodthirsty supporters. That could only mean there was more than one gunman. A few more shots rang out, striking Mrs. Dauson. She toppled over and appeared to be dead.

Clive began to black out due to the lack of oxygen, and as the darkness began to settle in, he stopped kicking. As he slowly drifted from consciousness, he suddenly felt himself drop to the ground, and a rush of air flooded his lungs. Coughing uncontrollably, he lay on the ground for a moment before someone dragged him to safety. Struggling to catch his breath, the bag was ripped from his head, revealing who had saved him.

It was a group of four people, their lower faces covered with bandanas. Clive looked around at all of them, not knowing if he should thank them or brace himself for a beating.

"Where am I?" Clive whispered, clutching his throat.

A tall man stood in a dark corner of the room, staring at the fugitive now on the run. He stood out from the others because he was wearing a gambler's hat and a long coat. "Back room of the saloon. We can hide out here until the coast is clear. It won't be long before that joke of a sheriff comes looking for whoever's responsible."

Clive mustered up the strength to sit up and said, "I don't think the barkeep will be okay with harboring fugitives in his storage room. That might be bad for business."

"Don't worry," the tall man replied. "I believe he won't have much of a problem with it." That was when the man stepped forward from the dark corner and began to take off his hat, which had been covering his face. It was the bartender that Clive had a brief conversation with days ago. It took Clive a moment to recognize him because he hadn't made much of an impression. "Name's Ralph," he said.

Confused and in shock, the only word that Clive could get out was, "Why?"

"Well, the three of us are the last people in this godforsaken town who haven't lost their damn minds. Between turning into those creatures or becoming the brainless sheep who bought into Daniel's mad justifications for letting them roam around, we're all this town has left. He thinks he's doing us all a favor when, in reality, he's just looking out for himself."

Ralph went on, "My business used to be booming from the number of people I'd get in the evenings, but ever since this town curfew was put into effect because of those monsters terrorizing us, I've been spending more money staying open than I'm making. Daniel Cody was a lousy, drunken farmer who blew his own opportunities and blamed his misfortune on the town for pushing him out of business. If he tells you otherwise, that's a bold-faced lie. He uses those beasts as a way to instill fear and run this town. Sheriff Freeman was an outstanding sheriff, and Daniel is a disgrace to the badge. So, we waited for the right moment to reclaim our town."

The rest of the crew pulled down their bandanas, revealing their faces.

"Jack over there has been here for ten years. He's a quiet man who's never caused any trouble. His cattle were all slaughtered one night by those vicious dogs, wolves, or whatever they are. His way of putting food on his family's table was wiped out in one night. He went to Daniel Cody to tell him what happened, and you know what our merciful leader said? 'It's a small price you pay for living in a utopia.' Can you believe it? Monsters running around, folks starving, and he has the gall to call it a utopia."

Ralph's focus shifted to the woman standing next to Jack. "That brings us to Bonnie over there. Her poor brother is one of those beasts that Daniel keeps in the basement. At night, he's a monster, killing everything in sight, and by day, he sits in a cage, barely clothed, being fed scraps just to keep him alive. Daniel promised her he would work tirelessly to find a cure and said he'd heard of someone out east who was working on a way to reverse the effects of a bite from one of those things. Bonnie bought into it at first, but now she understands there's no way of bringing him back. He's better off dead than being treated like an animal during the day and turning into one at night."

Ralph then nodded towards a man who towered over everybody. "Finally, we have the big man, Butch. He doesn't say much, but he's as strong as an ox and the only one of us who's come face-to-face with one of those creatures. No need to worry, though, he was never bitten. Clawed at? Sure. But we believe the sickness can only be transmitted through the bite of the beast. Could it be his brute strength that makes him a hell of an ally against those things, or maybe the massive hunting knife he always keeps on him that might even the odds against them? What he wants is simple: a life where he can walk outside without looking over his shoulder for something to lunge out at him."

Ralph finishes, "This town used to stand for something, a place where someone's hard work would be rewarded with a good life. If you had a family, there was no safer place. If you were young and single, the nightlife was like no other. It meant something to be from Moonlight Valley, and we're not going to let some identity thief rule with fear any longer. It ends tonight."

Chapter 12

The Town Meeting

"Alright, alright, everyone just relax," Daniel said. The townsfolk had been on edge due to the monsters that had taken up residence as of late. To ease the growing panic, Daniel had set up a town meeting at the saloon so folks could voice their concerns.

"First things first, I know you've all heard about Sheriff Freeman's unfortunate accident, so from this point on, I'll be accepting the role of sheriff."

"Wait, shouldn't we have an election to see who the people want as the new sheriff?" a voice called from the crowd.

"Who said that? Why don't you come on up so I can hear you better?" Daniel said, squinting toward the back of the saloon.

Sid Pierce, the town doctor, made his way to the front of the crowd so Daniel could hear him clearly.

"Ah, Doctor Pierce, I do apologize, but would you mind repeating yourself? I couldn't hear you all the way back there."

"I was saying, Daniel, that usually we have an election to decide who the sheriff will be. You know, just so the people are comfortable with who we're putting the responsibility for our safety in."

Daniel gave a little smirk. "Doctor Pierce, I very much support the democratic process. I mean, that's what this great country is built on. But time is something we have to be careful with. With these creatures terrorizing our home, we don't have the luxury of holding an election and leaving Moonlight Valley with nobody to defend it. You all deserve a fearless leader who will put your safety and your families' safety first. That's what I promise to do. I will make this town a place where everyone will not only feel safe but thrive. Even if that means we'll all need to make some sacrifices to get there. If you still have a problem with the lack of an election, I'll be glad to address your concerns after the meeting at the jail."

Sid nodded in agreement and fell back into the crowd. The mood in the saloon shifted slightly. There were many who didn't like that this failed rancher had seemingly appointed himself to the most important position in town, but honestly, nobody was willing to run against him. Who would knowingly put their life on the line in a battle they couldn't win, against an enemy that was a crime against nature? Daniel could feel he was starting to win the support of some of the townsfolk with his impassioned speech.

"Sheriff Freeman was a great man who you all elected because you felt he was the best person to hold the values of this town high. He proudly upheld them until his final breath. I gave him a proper, respectful burial a few mornings ago behind the jail, his home away from home. He put the quiet little town of Moonlight Valley on his back and brought it into better, more prosperous days. Since I share the same values as that fine man, I find it only appropriate that, from this point on, I go by Sheriff Freeman."

Daniel continued, "Now, I know this may seem odd to all of you, given that you've known me as Daniel for many years, but I feel that since everyone placed their respect in him, then I should command the same respect as well. I'd like to get the rest of this meeting underway, so if you could all raise your hands, we won't have anyone shouting over one another."

The crowd of people raised their hands.

"How about you over there? What's your question, honey?"

"Hi, my name is Bonnie."

"Hello there, Bonnie, what can I do for you?"

"Yes, the other night my brother was out late, and I haven't seen him since." Tears began to well up in her eyes, and her voice cracked. "He is never away from home this long without letting me know first. I know that he is still out there, I can feel it deep down. So, I guess I'm just asking for your help. Will you help find my brother and bring him home?"

"Oh, darlin', I'm sorry this has happened to you, and I assure you that I will work tirelessly to find your brother. I'll bring him home. You can count on that. That brings me to a rule that will definitely be controversial: nobody outside after sundown or before sunrise."

The people erupted in displeasure.

"You have got to be kidding me!" one voice shouted.

"What kind of life is that?" another townsperson called out.

"Now, you all are going to have to trust me. I know most of you can't wait for the workday to be over so you can enjoy the nightlife that Moonlight Valley has to offer, but this needs to be done. Those things only come around at night, so you all need to stay in for your own safety."

"That will kill my business!" Ralph yelled.

"Now, Ralph, I know you're upset, but—"

"You're damn right I'm upset! The nightlife in this town is the only way I can stay open. If you take that away, the saloon will go under."

Daniel raised his hands as a way to tell Ralph to calm down. "Ralph, I know this is going to sting for a while, but I promise it's not going to be forever. Remember, short-term sacrifices for long-term prosperity."

"You know, I've heard a lot of promises, but you haven't mentioned how you're going to get rid of these monsters," Ralph said, looking toward the others for support.

"I'm an honest man, and I'm going to say something that may worry some of you. I don't really know how to kill these things yet. What I do know is that they're not affected by normal bullets. I will find a way to exterminate those monsters, but just like everything else, it will take time."

"What about the farmers that are suffering?" a man said, raising his hand.

Daniel pointed at him and asked, "What's your name, sir?"

"The name is Jack."

"Besides not following instructions and yelling over everyone, what can I help you with, Jack?"

"I apologize. I'm just a little upset. My cattle have been getting slaughtered at night, and it's killing my business. My cows and sheep are ripped to shreds, some of them becoming nothing but a pile of bones by morning. What do you suggest I do? It's getting to the point I can't even afford to pay my farmhand, Butch."

Daniel thought for a minute. "You're gonna have to do a better job of locking up your barn and stable. As a matter of fact, you all should board up your windows and make sure your doors are locked tight. Who knows how strong these things are? I wouldn't take any chances. If you'll excuse me, I have a lot to do before sundown."

The new Sheriff Freeman made his way through the people and headed to the jail. The mood in the saloon was a mix of disappointment and faint hope. After hearing the promises of the new sheriff, many believed that he could be the man to lead Moonlight Valley out of darkness. Others weren't buying the slop Daniel was feeding them.

"This is bullshit," Ralph said, surrounded by a few people.

Bonnie heard him, turned, and said, "But he said he was going to find my brother."

The look on Ralph's face turned from anger to sadness. "I'm sorry, Bonnie, but I think he's just telling people what they want to hear. It really pains me to say this, but I'm afraid your brother might be gone."

Bonnie lowered her head in sorrow as Ralph placed his hand on her shoulder.

"Can you believe that bastard? 'Lock up your barn and stables better.' Absolute joke. This town is going to fall into financial ruin it'll never recover from. Not my fault he was a lousy rancher even before those monsters made their way into town."

"Say, since I have to close the saloon early now, why don't we all gather here and complain about our 'lovely' new sheriff? Just a way to blow off steam in a safe place, if you're interested. And don't worry, I'll make sure to kick you out before you become a snack for those things."

"Will the alcohol still be available even if the saloon is closed?" Jack asked.

Ralph chuckled. "Of course."

"I'll drink to that."

"How about you, Bon?"

Bonnie shook her head, still saddened that Daniel had lied to her just to get her to be quiet.

"Alright then, I'll see you all here later," Ralph said.

The four parted ways and went about their day. By daylight, Moonlight Valley seemed like any other town on the surface, but it wouldn't be long before the moon rose high and the seemingly safe streets turned into a feeding ground. The townsfolk began boarding up their windows, giving the place a deserted look.

Later that day, just as the sun was setting, Doctor Pierce made his way to the jail. He walked in to find Daniel at his desk.

"Daniel, you wanted to see me?"

Daniel looked up, displeased, and asked, "What did you just call me?"

"I'm sorry, Sheriff Freeman."

"That's more like it. Why don't you come on in and shut the door behind you."

Sid Pierce shut the door behind him and stood in front of Daniel's desk. The new sheriff sat back in his chair and folded his hands over his stomach.

"You seemed pretty upset that I announced myself as the new sheriff, but that was no reason to embarrass me the way you did earlier today."

"Embarrass you? I did no such thing. I just wanted the democratic way to be upheld; it's what this fine country was founded on."

Daniel smiled. "You know, I like you, Doc. That's why I wanted to show you something."

Doctor Pierce replied, "Whatever it is, can you make it quick? I'd like to be home before those things start roaming the streets." Daniel stood up, lit a lantern, and led the doctor downstairs to the basement.

"Where are we going?" the doctor asked.

"Just wait. I have something really special to show you, Doc."

Once down there, he stood in front of a cell with the lantern lowered, making it difficult for the doctor to see inside.

"You see, Doc, I have a friend who's been a bit under the weather lately, and I was hoping you'd be able to help him out."

Pierce's voice carried a tinge of hesitation. "Alright, let's take a look at him."

Nothing could prepare the doctor for the horror he was about to witness. Daniel raised the lantern to reveal a blood-covered Sheriff Freeman, looking mangled and breathing heavily. He wasn't alone, a young man was also in the cell, his body similarly smeared with blood. The former sheriff looked at the doctor, and with dried blood crusted around his mouth, whispered, "Help me."

"I-Is that the sheriff?" Doctor Pierce asked.

"No, silly. I'm the sheriff. That's the shell of the man who used to wear this badge."

"But you said he was dead and buried."

"What did you expect me to say? Was I supposed to tell people I had him locked up in the basement of the jail and that he turns into a monster at night?"

"Who is that other man in there?"

"That guy back there would be that lovely girl Bonnie's brother. I found him face down in the street a couple of days ago and threw him down here."

The doctor's face and tone were full of worry. "You can't do this, Daniel. It's unethical."

"Why can't you get this through your thick head? I'm Sheriff Freeman now. You keep disrespecting me for some reason, and that's why I'm officially terminating you from your position. I'm now accepting applications for a new doctor in Moonlight Valley."

"What? No, I love my job, and I'm good at it. The people of this town will start asking questions if I abruptly resign. I promise I won't say anything."

"Did you not see me at the town meeting this morning? All I have to do is come up with some bogus story about you leaving town for personal reasons, whether it's visiting a relative or whatever. As for now, get in the cell."

"What?"

Daniel took out his revolver and pointed it at the doctor. "You heard me. Get in the cell."

Daniel opened the cell door and shoved Pierce inside. Outside, the moon was high in the sky, transforming those who were infected into feral beasts. In the cell, the two blood-covered men dropped to the ground and began to convulse uncontrollably. Their mouths foamed, and their skin started to tear.

Doctor Pierce screamed and pleaded for Daniel to let him out. He shook the bars of the cell frantically, trying to escape. "PLEASE LET ME OUT!" he cried.

Behind him, where the two men had been lying, now stood two bloodthirsty monsters.

Daniel turned and walked back up the stairs as the doctor's screams filled the basement.

Chapter 13

A Man Drunk With Power

"Alright, if I know Daniel, he's going to want answers. So we don't have much time before he starts looking for them. Here's what we're going to do." Clive leaned in to hear the plan.

"We're going to do nothing."

"Nothing?"

"That's right. We're going to go about our day as we normally would. Nobody saw our faces, so we'll have no problem playing it cool. Clive, you're going to need to stay in here until tonight. Now, you said something about a basement full of monsters. Is there anything else you saw in the jail that might be useful?"

Before Clive had a chance to answer, they heard boots thudding on the hardwood floor of the saloon.

"Stay here and be quiet," Ralph whispered, grabbing a crate of whiskey bottles so he wouldn't seem suspicious to whoever was up front.

The sheriff was sitting at the bar. "Afternoon, Ralph."

Ralph set down the case of whiskey and replied, "Afternoon, Sheriff. Can I get you anything?"

"I'll have a beer if it isn't too much trouble."

Ralph filled the mug carefully, trying to keep a steady hand so as not to give himself away. He placed the mug of beer in front of the sheriff and proceeded to wipe down the counter.

"Say, Ralph, were you at the hanging earlier today?"

"No, sir. I was here getting everything ready for the day. I figured with a crowd of people gathering on the other side of the tracks, they were bound to want a drink after the festivities. Besides, I find the whole public murder a bit grotesque."

Daniel took a sip from his mug of beer. "You've always been a bit soft, haven't you, Ralph? If it were up to you, that lying, murderous Clive Holiday would have gotten a slap on the wrist followed by a pat on the back. Don't know if you heard, but he was saved from being hanged by a merry band of outlaws who are also guilty of murdering a few people in this fine town. The bad news is, we're already running low on townsfolk thanks to those monsters, and I have an investigation to conduct. So I don't have any time to bury them. I'm going to have to leave them in the street, where those monsters—the murderers, not the wolves—will have a constant reminder of the carnage they inflicted."

Ralph finished wiping down the counter and replied, "Damn shame, Sheriff."

The sheriff took another sip of his beer. "You know, the funny thing is, I'm not much of a drinker, but after the day I've had, almost being killed, I couldn't think of another way to relax. I'll tell you this: before sundown, I'll go door to door and interrogate everyone who was at the hanging today. When I find Clive Holiday and whoever is responsible for helping him escape, I will personally hang all of them outside tonight so those monsters can eat them from the feet up."

Daniel stood up, thanking Ralph for the drink and buying a whole bottle of whisky to drink later on his own. Ralph made sure that Daniel was gone before going back to the storage closet and letting everyone know that the coast was clear. Everyone, except for Clive, exited the saloon and went on with their day.

As the day went on, the sheriff's next stop was the general store, where thirty-three-year-old Colt McDowery was stocking shelves. Colt was a very unassuming man. He had big, round glasses and always wore suspenders. His build was what you would describe as pipsqueakish.

"Howdy, Colt," Daniel said with a tip of his hat.

"Oh, hey, Sheriff. Sorry, I can't see much because I lost my glasses this afternoon. Is there anything I can get for you? I can give you a special on that jerky you like."

"No thanks, Colt. By chance, did you lose your glasses due to the commotion at the hanging earlier today?"

"As a matter of fact, I did, and I have never been more terrified in my entire life. As soon as the shooting started, I ran as fast as I could to safety. I tripped and fell, knocking off my glasses, but I couldn't go back for them. I hid behind the doctor's office until everything seemed to calm down."

The sheriff reached into his dungarees pocket and took out Colt's shattered glasses.

"You found them! Geez, they sure have seen better days, but I guess I'll have to do without until I'm able to get a replacement pair. Thank you for returning them to me, Sheriff."

"You see, I've been asking around, and there have been some witnesses who said that the shooting started in the general direction you happened to be standing in. That, combined with your broken glasses, doesn't exactly put you in the best light."

"W-W-What do my broken glasses have to do with anything?"

"To a lesser sheriff, it would probably seem like a mere coincidence. They'd buy your story of tripping and running away to hide. I have to tell you, though, those lousy bums don't have an ounce of what I have, which sets me apart from everyone else. The way the glasses broke, combined with the awful aim of the shooters, tells me they were inexperienced. So let me tell you what I know so you don't continue to lie to me. You've never aimed a gun before and, like a fool, held it too close to your face. The recoil of the gun was so strong that it knocked your glasses off, and the bullet missed its mark. Well, it missed me—Mrs. Dauson wasn't so lucky. But don't worry, she's back in a cell and will be fine at sundown. I mean, as fine as one can be, given that she will turn into a wolf-like creature when the moon arises.

Daniel took his revolver from his holster and pointed it straight at Colt.

"But why would I do that? I like the way everything is. I have a beautiful wife, Sally, and three lovely children, whom you've met. Do you remember, Daniel? I would never do anything to jeopardize that!" Colt said, as tears ran down his cheeks.

"What did you just say?"

"I said I would never do anything to jeopardize—"

BANG!

Daniel shot Colt, who dropped to the ground like a ton of bricks. Blood began to pool underneath him as he reached up toward the sheriff, grabbing at the shelves and knocking over canned goods. The sheriff stood over him for what felt like minutes, studying the dying man.

"The name is Sheriff Freeman," he said before exiting the store.

Daniel walked about ten feet from the store before turning around to face it. He reached into his coat, pulling out the bottle of whisky he'd bought from the saloon. Then he slipped his hand into the back pocket of his dungarees, took out a cloth and a match, and set to work. He opened the bottle, stuffed the rag into its neck, then struck the match on the sole of his snakeskin boot and lit the rag. He hurled the bottle as hard as he could at the general store, turning the quiet shop into an inferno. It wasn't long before the whole place was ablaze. A subtle smirk crossed his face, pleased with what he'd just done.

A few of the residents of the town came running outside with buckets of water, trying to extinguish the flames. They worked around the sheriff, who just stood there admiring the blaze before turning and speaking in a loud, booming voice.

"Let this be a lesson to anyone who not only questions my leadership but also tries to take my life. I will not be intimidated, nor will I lay down and let what I built be threatened."

Back at the saloon, Ralph ran outside through the double doors to see what all the commotion was about. He looked down at the other end of town to see black smoke from the fire filling the sky. As he was standing there, he saw the sheriff walk past him.

"Everything alright, Sheriff?"

"I'm gonna get them all, every last one of them," Daniel muttered to himself, walking into the jail.

Ralph decided to take a trip to the other end of town to see what exactly had caught on fire. When he arrived, he was met with grown men standing with tears in their eyes and their hats over their hearts, circling the general store. The folks were unable to contain the flames, so the fire roared on.

It didn't take long before Sally and her three children pushed through the crowd of men. "Is Colt alright? Did he make it out?" she asked. When all of them dropped their heads to avoid eye contact, she dropped to her knees, screaming and clutching her children.

"What happened?" Ralph asked one of the men.

The man turned to him and said, "The sheriff has gone mad and told us this was an example of what happens if anyone crosses him. You don't actually think Colt was one of the people trying to kill the sheriff, do you? I've known him for many years, and he would never even hurt a fly."

Ralph, overcome with guilt, turned pale as a ghost. He headed back to the saloon and poured himself a shot of whisky. He walked back into the storage room where Clive was and asked, "What was in that jail that could help us kill Daniel?"

"Kill Daniel? First, I'll start off by saying how grateful I am that you and your friends saved me from getting hanged, but I don't know if you've noticed that you tried doing that already. The more I try to help, the more shit I seem to find myself in. So, here's my plan: I'm going to stay right here until the sun goes down. Then you'll come and get me, and I'll hop the train when it passes through tonight. I'm going to leave any talk about werewolves and that crazy sheriff behind."

"So that's it, huh? You're just going to run from your problems? I hate to break it to you, but what's happening right here is bigger than you. It's bigger than me. We're talking about saving humanity here. What if one of those things makes its way to a bigger city? After that, it would only be a matter of time before the country is overrun with those monsters."

"You think those things are confined to just this town?" Clive began to yell. "I don't know if you've noticed, but that train of yours that runs through the center of this town is the direct pipeline for spreading those things throughout the country."

"What do you mean?"

"Before I got here, I encountered one of those things on the train I hopped back in Dodge City."

"That can't be true. I've seen those things roaming around at night. Once the train comes barreling through here, they scurry away. Don't know if it's the blinding headlight or the deafening whistle, but as soon as it gets close, those things head for the shadows. It could also be that they have the brains of wild animals, so they see the train as a bigger predator. They probably realize that if a werewolf goes head-to-head with a thousand-ton piece of metal moving thirty miles an hour, the train's going to win every time. Monster or not, the laws of the jungle still apply."

"So, what are you thinking? One of the people here jumped the train after getting bitten, or someone saw how life was here and jumped the train?"

Ralph thought for a moment. "While possible, it's highly unlikely. The train is a single-track operation, which means in the afternoon it passes through the town in one direction, sometimes stopping for Daniel's special deliveries, and just before sunrise, it passes through in the opposite direction. The nearest station is about four hours by train, so I'd add another few hours by horseback. As for the ones that wake up in random places with ripped or no clothes, going to the doctor or sheriff to see what the problem is would be their first thought."

"The sheriff did say he was watching the doctor's office to see the line of people standing out there so he could eventually throw them in a cell underneath the jail."

"Did he take you down there? How many did you see?" Ralph asked urgently.

"I don't really remember. Why?"

"The number of people I have seen disappear in this town has to be in the mid to high twenties, which means those people are going somewhere. But where?"

"You think the sheriff killed them? Maybe they questioned his way of running this nightmare of a town, and he fed them to his little pets down there."

"The sheriff only resorts to murder if he sees it as an example to keep everyone in line. It wouldn't surprise me if he sacrifices some of these fine folks to weaponize them and use them to rule over the rest of us. I need to figure out a way of stopping him, but I need you to tell me what was in that jail."

Clive struggled to remember. "Not much, really. Just those monsters downstairs, and oh, a lot of explosives."

"Explosives?"

"Yeah, he said he was using them to expand the basement of the jail because the rate of people turning is too great for the space he has down there."

"If that's the case, then where did all of those people from town go who went missing?"

They both sat for a while in silence, thinking about what the answer was. Staring blankly at the wall, a memory came to Clive.

"I didn't think much about it, but after they brought in the crates filled with explosives, they brought out larger crates. I don't know what was in them."

"How big are we talking, Clive?" urged Ralph.

"Pretty big. I mean, they each required a guy at both ends to carry them out to the train."

"Enough to fit a body?"

"I mean, yeah, but why?"

"That son of a bitch. He's been shipping those things off to the next town."

"Wait, what? You mean to tell me that they were putting people in those boxes and bringing them to the next town?"

Ralph looked Clive in the eye and said, "That is exactly what I'm saying. And who knows if the crates stayed in that town or stayed on the train and were brought somewhere else? I need to get the rest of the crew together. It looks like we need to pay the yellow-belly sheriff a visit and see what he has to say for himself."

Ralph rounded up Bonnie, Jack, and Butch, all sporting their disguises from earlier this afternoon. Ralph held out a hat and bandana for Clive as if asking if he was in or out. Clive stared at them for a minute, thinking about how crazy all of this was. He could just make his escape and forget about all of this. Then his mind shot back to the man he accidentally killed in Dodge City and Paul Kelp, who had the same goal as this ragtag group: to save the ones they cared most for. He looked up at Ralph and replied, "I'm going to need a gun."

Ralph smirked at Clive and gave him a nod, handing him the disguise. Ralph knew the sheriff wasn't going home tonight, not on the day someone had almost shot him dead in front of the town. They waited until dusk and stormed over to the jail.

Chapter 14

A Wolf in Wolf's Clothing

CRASH! Ralph kicked in the jailhouse door, followed by his posse. Daniel shot up from his chair and aimed his revolver at them. His hand was shaking from the adrenaline, or maybe it was from the half-drunk bottle of whisky on his desk. The four of them all had their weapons drawn, pointing at Daniel.

"Not so fast, Daniel. There are five of us and one of you. I reckon even if you manage to shoot one of us, the rest will have you lying in a pool of your own blood before you even have a chance to blink," Ralph said.

The sheriff lowered his gun and sat back down in his chair. He grabbed the bottle of whisky and poured himself another shot. He drank it, wiped his face on his sleeve, and said, "Well, I guess you got me. So you're the cowards who tried to kill me today during the hanging, right? So that's it? You're going to kill me without even showing me who any of you are? Come on, grant a dying man a wish and show me your faces," the sheriff said in a disturbingly cheery tone.

The five outlaws lowered their bandanas, revealing their faces. Shocked and confused, the sheriff couldn't help but chuckle.

"Ralph, you tried to kill me? But why? And not only that—why would you help this murderer, who deserves to die for his crimes?"

"The only one who deserves to die for the crimes they've committed is you, Daniel. You've killed innocent civilians and used those monsters to rule over our fine town."

"This fine town has forgotten about people like you and me and left us out here to die. It chose wealth and prosperity over the residents that made it what it was," Daniel said, pouring himself another glass of whiskey.

Ralph walked over to the desk and removed Daniel's revolver from the table. He handed it to Clive, who placed it in his holster.

"Have you not looked around the town lately, or are you too blinded by your own pride to see what is actually going on here? You are the one who is destroying this town. Just look at what you did, you killed Colt and burned down his shop."

Daniel gave a matter-of-fact smile and said, "What's wrong? Are you upset that I got to one of yours before he was able to get to me?"

"Listen, you lunatic, Colt was never one of ours. He was a fine man with a wife and three children, and you gunned him down like a wild animal. Not only that, you set fire to his shop, so his poor wife has no way of supporting herself and her three children."

"But I found his broken glasses at the scene, and witnesses said they saw the shooting coming from the direction where he was standing. So, if he wasn't guilty of trying to kill me, then that makes you responsible for his death. Absolutely disgusting, you let an innocent man die because you were too cowardly to come to me face-to-face and do the job like grown adults. So instead, I had to go down to that general store and make that poor man beg me not to shoot him. It was actually pretty sad, if you ask me. But hey, you're the ones who killed Colt. I was just carrying out an investigation; you could call it following a lead."

Clive, having heard enough of what he was listening to, burst out, "You should be ashamed of yourself. These people look to you to keep them safe, but instead, this is what you do. It's sad that in a town full of werewolves, the biggest monster sits behind that desk."

Daniel stood up from his chair and locked eyes with Clive.

"That's rich coming from a man who should be six feet deep right now. Did you tell your newfound friends about what you've done? What exactly are you running from? Maybe something you did back in Dodge City? That's right, you'd be surprised by the things you hear as a sheriff. Just yesterday, I got a letter warning the town about a fugitive who killed a man back in Dodge City."

Everybody looked at one another, then at Clive.

"Oh, did you all know that you rescued a man who left someone lying in a pool of their own blood just to steal a few bucks? The truth is, we are all monsters and capable of unspeakable things; it's whether or not you act on it that separates us. And sometimes it takes a monster to keep other monsters at bay. Maybe instead of whining and crying, you should all thank me. I don't know if you've noticed, but I have a pretty healthy following. So, what exactly are you looking for? An apology? If so, I'm sorry. I'm sorry that you don't have what it takes to seize an opportunity like I did and lead this town back to where it used to be."

Bonnie interrupted, "Back to where it used to be? What about my brother? You promised me a way to bring him back, but instead, you keep him prisoner down in that basement in unspeakable conditions."

Daniel, now leaning over his desk, rolled his eyes and turned to Bonnie. "Honey, we both know the only antidote for whatever he has is a nice little silver bullet to the head, and after the little stunt you pulled this afternoon, I'm inclined to go down there and do it right in front of you. Actually, I have a better idea. Maybe I will bring you down there and put you in the cell with him. It seems like a good time for a family reunion."

Daniel took a step back and extended his arms. "I'm supposed to be intimidated by a failed rancher, a dumb field worker, a gullible woman, a man whose saloon is on its last leg, and a murderer?"

It was now Jack's turn to speak up. "Failed rancher? It was your monsters who killed my cattle. I came to you for help, and you just ignored me. I went out of business. The real Sheriff Freem—"

"You came to me looking for a handout. Do you think anyone came to my rescue after I lost my farm? Let me save you some time: the answer is no. I waited, made my move, and now look at me, the most powerful man in Moonlight Valley. As for that lousy excuse for a sheriff, he probably would have bailed you out, but that's why he is downstairs in a cage right now. Ain't no place in this town for a soft sheriff," Daniel said, interrupting Jack.

With his blood boiling, Clive began to yell, "We know you've been transporting people out of town in those big crates! You load them onto the train that comes in the afternoon, and then it drops them off in the next town over before sundown. But why would you do such a thing?"

"Aren't you a nosy little murderer? Well, since this appears to be the end of the line for me, I might as well come clean. You're right, the plan was to have those crates delivered by sundown to the next town over. Either the infected folks would turn there and the monsters would be on the loose, or they'd be loaded on another train bound far from here. My reach would be felt across this great land. Those poor, ill-equipped people would have no choice but to come looking for refuge here. Or maybe I let a little more time pass, go there preaching my knowledge, and claim I'm the only one who can keep them safe. They will have no choice but to let me run this town, and who knows, maybe one day I'll run this country. 'President Freeman' has a nice ring to it," boasted Daniel.

The five of them could not believe what they were hearing. Did this madman actually plan to set those creatures loose across the country? One thing was true: he had bought into his own hysteria and believed his actions would not only save the nation but also usher in better days.

"As for the judge from the other day, he knows about these creatures walking among us and fully believes in my plan. That is why you never stood a chance, well, that and some extra cash to play stupid."

As the psychopath continued to ramble, the five of them didn't notice a man quietly creeping in through the jailhouse front door, cradling his double-barrel shotgun. He carefully lifted his weapon and fired. *BAM!* The blast from the gun was so strong that it knocked him back slightly, but not before the bullets struck Jack. The four of them looked down at the former rancher, who was gone before he even hit the ground, a gaping hole where his stomach used to be.

They all turned to the man in the doorway and opened fire. By the time they were done with their deadly barrage, the man had more holes in him than flesh on his body. They turned back toward the desk where the sheriff had been, but he was gone. He must have crawled under the desk and made a run for it. Knowing there was no way he could escape through the only door to the jail—the same one where his henchman lay torn apart by bullets—they knew the only place he could have gone was down to the basement.

The four of them didn't have much time to think because more of the sheriff's goons opened fire outside the jail. One was perched on the roof of the post office, and another was hiding behind a parked carriage.

"Bonnie and Butch, can you take care of them if Clive and I go after the sheriff downstairs?"

Bonnie and Butch both nodded and ran outside, guns blazing, taking cover behind wooden barrels filled with water. Clive and Ralph then headed down to the basement in pursuit of Daniel. They made it about halfway down the stairs before shots rang out from the darkness. The sheriff had gotten hold of a revolver he had stashed down there and opened fire.

Clive and Ralph returned fire into the darkness, unsure of what they were hitting. Remembering the explosives stored below, Clive yelled for Ralph to cease fire. Oddly enough, the shooting from the darkness stopped as well. Clive rushed back up the stairs to grab a lit oil lamp from the sheriff's desk.

Outside, Bonnie and Butch were still engaged in a firefight with a few of the brainwashed townsfolk. Bonnie took down the man on top of the post office with a shot clean between the eyes. If the gunshot didn't kill him, then the fall from the roof to the hard earth certainly did.

As the one hiding behind the carriage paused to reload, Butch charged, lifting him into the air and slamming him to the ground, knocking the wind from his lungs. He then used the butt of his revolver to brutally smash the man's face, turning it into a mess of blood and bone.

Sweating and splattered with blood, Butch walked back over to the jail to stand guard with Bonnie.

Downstairs, Clive led the way, the lamp's flickering light revealing the people in the cages. Most looked like they hadn't seen sunlight in weeks. Mrs. Dauson lay motionless from her fatal gunshot wound. Clive turned the lamp toward a trail of blood that led to Daniel, who was sitting there clutching his shoulder, blood from a bullet wound seeping through his shirt.

"Well, it looks like you got me," Daniel said, followed by a fit of coughing.

Ralph began to inspect the bullet wound in Daniel's shoulder. "Well, by the looks of it, that appears to be just a flesh wound, which is very unlucky for you."

"And why's—AHHH!"

Before Daniel could finish his sentence, Ralph drove his thumb deep into the wound.

Just then, the prisoners collapsed to the ground, shaking and screaming in pain. Clive knew what this meant, he'd seen it a handful of times before, but he could never get used to it. This being Ralph's first time witnessing such a horrific transformation, he instinctively shielded his eyes, though nothing could block out the bloodcurdling screams.

A few of the prisoners had already caught stray bullets from the shootout moments earlier, but that didn't seem to affect them now. Mrs. Dauson, who was presumed dead from her gunshot wound, was now convulsing violently on the ground. Their skin began to tear open in unison, and their faces stretched and elongated into grotesque snouts. Their yellowish-brown teeth sharpened into jagged fangs.

Clive turned the lamp away, unable to stomach more of the nightmarish sight. By the time he looked back, the transformation was complete. A dozen pairs of glowing yellow eyes pierced through the darkness.

The smell of blood from Daniel's arm was like bait to the monsters; they leaped at the bars of the cells, growling and frothing at the mouth. Ralph raised his rifle and started firing into the cells. *BANG! BANG! BANG!* The shots echoed through the basement. Bonnie and Butch came running downstairs, but when Clive turned the lamp to reveal the monsters, they stopped dead in their tracks. Clive then turned the lamp to reveal the pile of explosives Daniel had stashed against the back wall.

"That's enough explosives to take out all of us," Bonnie said.

Ralph continued to shoot at the werewolves, making them angrier and more frenzied.

"I guess not everyone is up to date on how to kill a werewolf—AHHH!" Daniel teased, before Clive shoved his thumb into the hole in his shoulder like Ralph had previously done.

Ralph stopped shooting and turned to Clive. "What does he mean?"

"The only way to kill one of those is with a silver bullet or by destroying its body. Shooting at them with your rifle is just provoking them," Clive replied.

That's when Ralph had an idea. He aimed his rifle at the explosives, cocked it, and—Clive grabbed the barrel, trying to wrestle the gun away. The two struggled for a moment before the gun went off while it was pointed at the ceiling.

"Are you out of your mind?!" Clive screamed. "You can't shoot those explosives, we'll all die!"

"It'd be worth it if that meant taking out all of these abominations and that joke of a sheriff!" Ralph yelled back.

They both turned to the wall where Daniel sat, but he was no longer there. Clive turned the lamp to the cells to reveal Daniel standing in front of one of them, a menacing grin on his face. He said, "Remember, there is a monster in all of us."

Ralph aimed his rifle at him and—*click*— it was out of ammo. Daniel thrust his wounded arm into the cell. It took less than a second for the werewolves to smell the blood and lunge, tearing his arm to shreds. Daniel screamed in agony, but it only lasted for about a minute before Clive shot him, ending his misery.

The four of them sank down against the wall opposite the cells, exhausted and trying to think of a plan. The sheriff problem had been dealt with, but now there was the issue of man-eating werewolves to contend with.

"Do you think we should just pack up and ride away to another town now?" Bonnie suggested.

"We didn't do all of this just to abandon Moonlight Valley. Now, we might be four of the very few people left in this town, but we still have monsters roaming around up there and in here. However, I first have to ask Clive if what Daniel said was true," Ralph said.

Clive tilted his head in confusion. "What do you mean?"

"Did you kill that man back in Dodge City like Daniel said?"

Clive took a moment and let out a deep sigh. "Yes, I did. I'd like to say, and I have said, that it wasn't my fault, but it was all my fault. The same pressure that drove Daniel mad is the same pressure that drove me to start robbing people at gunpoint. I was a farmer just like he was, and the town began to expand, bringing in more competition and driving me out of business."

Clive continued to explain, "Unfortunately, one day, the man I was robbing decided enough was enough and tried to wrestle the gun away from me. One thing led to another, the gun went off, and he died. After that, I was on the run, and this nightmare hasn't ended. And before you ask me, there hasn't been a day that goes by that I haven't thought about him or the moment the light in his eyes went out. I truly am sorry. I just wish I could tell him that. I guess that lunatic was right about one thing: 'There is a monster in all of us.'"

It was at that moment that the lifeless body of Daniel began to convulse on the ground, and he let out the most disturbing screams any of them had ever heard. His arm, mostly nothing but torn tissue and bone at this point, was now replaced with a hulking limb covered in fur. At the end of his arms, his hands doubled in size and turned into paws with claws capable of ripping the skin off anyone who got in his way. His ears began to sharpen as he continued to shake uncontrollably.

"NO, NO, NO! I thought we killed him. How is he still alive?" Ralph yelled.

"I guess we were too late. By the time I shot him, he had been bitten by the ones in the cage, and the infection was already in his body," Clive answered.

Daniel continued to transform into a monster, now fully covered in hair, and his feet extended into paw-like shapes. Butch thought it would have been a good idea to shoot him, but it was no use. The now fully transformed Daniel stood up, facing the opposite direction from the four of them, and slowly began to turn around. He was taller and stronger than any other werewolf they had seen in the cell or walking the streets. He let out a roar so loud that it threatened to burst their eardrums. The four of them turned and ran, leaving the lamp behind, stumbling through the dark as they made their way upstairs. The monster whirled toward the cells, ripping the doors off their hinges and freeing the other werewolves. The hunt was on.

Chapter 15

Like Sheep to the Slaughter

Clive, Ralph, Bonnie, and Butch ran as fast as they could up the stairs from the basement, tripping over almost every step in the darkness. Close to a dozen beasts nipped at their heels, ready to sink their teeth into any one of them. Echoes of gunfire filled the jail, and while their bullets could only slow the monsters, it did buy them precious time to escape.

"Where are we going to go?" Clive asked.

Being outside at this hour was almost as dangerous as being in the jail basement. Ralph led the way, bringing the group to an old storm cellar behind the saloon. Ralph ripped open the wooden doors as the beasts drew near. Clive and Butch fired their weapons a few more times at the monsters, causing them to roar in pain, but only angering them further.

As they went down the stairs into the dark abyss of the storm cellar, Ralph closed the double doors behind them, but before he could secure the second door, one of the beasts reached its paw-like hand down and grabbed him by the face. Ralph screamed in terror as the beast tried to get a better grip.

The remaining three grabbed and pulled at the hairy beast's arm to no avail.

"Help!" Ralph cried. "Hel—" Just as he was yelling, one of the beast's claws slipped into his mouth, giving Ralph an opportunity to break free. He bit down as hard as he could and pulled his head back. The skin on the beast's appendage stretched as blood spurted from it. With one final jolt, Ralph fell to the ground while the beast let out a roar of pain, releasing him. He stood up and spat the finger onto the ground.

"Quick! Grab the chain and lock over there and secure the door handles!" Ralph demanded.

Clive and Bonnie ran to the side of the storm cellar that was illuminated only by the moonlight shining through the slats of the door. They did their best to wrap the chains around the handles while Butch used his strength to keep the doors closed as the threats outside struggled violently to get in. Just as Bonnie finished securing the chain, the doors ripped open, and one of the beasts snatched her by the arm. She struggled to break free, but it was no use.

Butch and Clive gripped her legs and pulled with all their might, but the beast was too strong. Ralph shot the monster multiple times, but it only furthered the werewolf's rage. All Bonnie could do was scream as its grip tightened.

She looked up at the werewolf holding her and locked eyes with it. Through the fury and rabidness, she realized it wasn't just one of the beasts, it was her brother. The same one Daniel had locked in the basement. She whispered, "I'm sorry. I should have protected you." Then she kicked her legs free from Clive and Butch, but before she could escape, the beast sank its razor-sharp teeth into her head, causing her to scream as it ran off, carrying her in its mouth.

"BONNIE!" the men screamed.

Bonnie's sacrifice bought the men enough time to shut the doors, wrap the chain around them, and lock them. Clive collapsed to the ground, weeping from the trauma he had just witnessed, while Ralph lit the lamps that hung on the walls of the storm cellar. All Butch could do was stare at the doors as they rattled from the monsters trying to get in. Fortunately for them, Daniel, or what was formerly Daniel, didn't see where they ran, otherwise, he would have ripped the doors right off their hinges.

Ralph finished lighting the lamps, blood still running down his jaw from biting off the werewolf's finger, and said, "No time to rest. We need a plan."

"But... Bonnie..." Clive could barely get the words out.

"Bonnie is gone. She died trying to put an end to all of this."

"There is no use. We're all dead. Now it's just a waiting game to see when the next one of us is taken out by one of those things," Clive muttered in a defeated tone.

Ralph looked at Clive with disgust and anger.

"So, what do you suggest we do then, Clive? Stay down here and starve to death? Or better yet, we wait for that massive beast Daniel turned into to finally come around and break in here, killing us all? Yes, Jack and Bonnie were victims of those beasts and the maniacs who were blinded by Daniel's preaching, but don't let their deaths be for nothing. Who knows how many of those things are out there around the town? Hell, if one made its way to the coast, this could be a worldwide issue. What I do know is that there is an army of those hairy bastards just begging for us to destroy them. Now, what do you say we stop feeling sorry for ourselves and come up with an idea to end this once and for all?"

Clive stood up, wiping his eyes, and nodded in agreement. The doors of the cellar rattled as the beasts tried desperately to gain entry. Butch was still on watch, gun in hand. He was strong and could probably hold his own against one of them, but who knows how many were on the other side of that door. In a rare moment, he turned toward the two men and said, "Whatever you come up with, you're going to need to make it quick. I don't know how long these doors will hold."

"Alright, what do we know about killing those things up there?"

"In all of the research Paul did, the documents clearly stated that the only way to kill a werewolf is with a silver bullet or by destroying the body."

"Okay, can we shoot these damn things with a silver bullet in the leg or arm to cure them, to cure the curse?"

Clive took a minute before destroying Ralph's last glimmer of hope. "Unfortunately, the ones we know and love are gone now, stuck in the misery of becoming flesh-craving monsters by night."

"But where are we going to get silver bullets? If the blacksmith isn't already one of those things up there, then that wannabe sheriff definitely had him in his back pocket."

Clive racked his brain, then under his breath he said, "'I had the blacksmith make several of these beauties.'"

"What?" Ralph questioned.

"Daniel had the blacksmith make silver bullets from an old pocket watch he took from me when he threw me in jail."

"Where are they?"

"That's the tricky part. They're back at the jail in his desk drawer. How about we wait until morning, sneak up there, and grab them instead of risking our skin tonight."

Ralph looked disappointed. "You want to wait until tomorrow, when Daniel and practically the whole town will be looking for us? Like I said before, Clive, this ends tonight."

"I'd rather take my chances with real humans trying to kill me than with real-life monsters trying to eat me."

"Ah, real-life monsters such as yourself?"

"Pardon me?"

"Did the man you shot back in Dodge City have the choice to wait until it was safer for him to get robbed and shot dead in the middle of the street?"

"I did what I needed to do in order to survive, just like everyone else in this damn town, and I have to live with my sins every day. What about you?"

"What about me?"

"You stand there all self-righteous, like none of these folks' blood is on your hands. Bonnie, Jack, and countless other deaths could have been avoided if you had tried to get help."

"Tried to get help? I'm struggling to remember. Did that go so well for you? You want me to ride to the next town over and ramble about giant wolf-people wandering the streets at night? They'd laugh me out of town before I could even finish. And I also can't remember, but I think the four of us are the only reason you're even still alive."

"You should have let me hang. I was ready to pay for what I've done."

"You think dying was going to be an adequate payment for taking a life? No, your penance is going to be far more difficult than that. You need to stand for something instead of lying down and waiting for death to call your name. If that is what you truly want, I'll have Butch open that door, and you can walk right out there with those beasts. I reckon you wouldn't even last five minutes before becoming their next meal."

Clive didn't move, but clenched his fists.

"That's what I thought. Just spineless and yellow—"

Clive punched Ralph right in the face, sending him to the ground. Ralph got back up, gave a bloody smirk, and lunged at Clive, knocking him down. The two rolled around on the hard cellar floor before Butch walked over and separated them. They continued to scratch and claw at each other, even though Clive knew that Butch's loyalty lay with Ralph, and he couldn't take them both in a fight.

"Knock it off!" Butch yelled before drawing his gun on Clive.

Ralph, blood pouring from his lip and his clothes dusty, became irate. "That's it! We risk our lives trying to save you, and this is how you repay us? I should have had Butch put a bullet right between your eyes. Better yet, Butch, why don't you unchain the doors and let those monsters down here to kill us all? If Clive had his way, we'd all throw our hands up right now and accept that this is it. You know what? Allow me."

Ralph retrieved the key from his pocket and headed toward the doors.

"Are you mad?" Clive asked.

"I'm not mad, I've finally seen what kind of man Clive Holiday is. He's willing to do whatever it takes to survive, as long as the one with everything to lose is him."

"Screw you!"

"Tell me I'm wrong. How many people did you rob back home? How many fine folks did you hold up and make feel like their lives were in danger, that any sudden move could be the difference between a bad day and their last day? How do we know it was only one person you killed? Maybe three, if you count the poor doctor and his wife."

"That was self-defense," Clive interjected.

164

"Even so, it seems wherever you go, death follows you. If you're not going to help us, this is where you get off."

Just as Ralph put the key in the lock, Butch yelled, "That's it!" then pointed his gun at Ralph.

"What are you doing, Butch?" Ralph snapped.

"Put the key back in your pocket and back away from the lock."

"What? You're protecting him after everything we've been through? After risking our lives for this ungrateful worm?"

Ralph tucked the key back into his pocket before returning to stand beside Clive. "Usually, I stand back and let you do all the talking because, honestly, Ralph, you're a lot smarter than me. Everything we've done has come from a place of helping the good people of this town. But I gotta tell you, right now, the way you're speaking and acting, you sound a lot like Daniel."

"What the hell did you just say?"

"Listen to yourself. You were going to open those doors and send Clive outside to those monsters. That's exactly what that fake sheriff would do to anyone who disagreed with him. You've spent so much time trying to figure out how to take him down, living in his head, that you've become him. Ralph, I know you're upset because it seems like everyone we love keeps dying, but you have to understand Clive is just scared. You can't really blame him; none of this is normal. You've always been good to me, Ralph, because you are a good man standing up for what you believe in."

Ralph hung his head in shame because he knew what Butch, who often replied with one-word answers and grunts, was saying was true. Even he couldn't believe some of the things he was saying or doing, the countless people Daniel had sent to those monsters as examples of what would happen if anyone opposed his way of running things, like sheep to the slaughter.

"Now, if we're done fighting and feeling sorry for ourselves, we need to come up with a plan because I'm not living another day in fear of those things. Not to mention, once the sun rises, the sheriff and his goons will also be on the hunt for us. Come on, what do you say?"

Clive was the first to nod in approval, and Ralph gave a thumbs-up, keeping his head down in embarrassment. The three took some time to conjure a plan, all the while monsters roamed the earth above them. The cellar doors had stopped rattling, indicating that the werewolves had lost interest in pursuing them or maybe a more easily obtainable prey had caught their eye.

Clive spoke up first, "Alright, we know we need to get to the jail to fetch those silver bullets, but how do we get to them? Also, even if we get them, I can assure you there won't be enough to take out all of them. There's probably only enough to load a single revolver."

"Is there anyone left alive up there who might be able to make more for us?" Butch asked.

Ralph shook his head. "There's a reason this town only ever had one blacksmith. Also, the few people up there who haven't turned are far too afraid to come outside and risk being eaten alive by those things."

The three continued to pitch ideas until one came to Clive so outrageous that he wondered if he was a genius or completely out of his mind.

"Butch, do you still have a large hunting knife on you?"

"Never leave home without it."

"What is the handle made of?"

"I don't know... silver, I think. Why?"

"Maybe the only way to get past them is to become one of them."

Chapter 16

Becoming the Monster

"Wait, you want Butch to do what?" Ralph said in disbelief.

Clive repeated himself as if what he was saying weren't outrageous.

Butch, without hesitation, said, "Alright, I'll do it."

Ralph stood in shock at his willingness, and Clive, despite proposing such a plan, was equally shocked at Butch's lack of objections. They knew they needed to act now before it became inevitable that more werewolves or the massive beast that Daniel had turned into could sniff them out.

Ralph and Clive approached the locked doors of the cellar, then looked back at Butch, who gave a nod of approval. Ralph unlocked the chains on the doors, and Clive opened the doors just slightly to survey the surroundings. About a yard from the entrance of the cellar stood one of the beasts, facing the opposite direction, as if guarding it to ensure nobody else tried to seek refuge inside. Clive shut the door gently and signaled to Butch that one was about three feet away. Butch let out one last heavy sigh before Clive and

Ralph silently counted down from three. *Three... two... one...*

Clive and Ralph swung the doors open, and Butch rushed out toward the beast. He grabbed it by the neck from behind and dragged it into the storm cellar before the other two closed and locked the doors behind them. They knew they couldn't have killed the beast by choking it out, but the lack of oxygen would certainly cause it to pass out. The werewolf frantically swung its arms and kicked its legs, trying to escape Butch's grasp. It snapped at the air in a desperate attempt to defend itself. The beast managed to get its feet underneath it before standing up, lifting Butch off the ground. He tried his best to hold on. It whipped its head back and forth in a violent fashion.

"Quick, grab its legs!" Butch yelled.

Ralph and Clive each grabbed hold of one of the monster's legs, causing it to fall back to the ground. It continued to fight for a couple more minutes before fading into unconsciousness. Butch held on a while longer until he was sure it was out cold. As it lay there with its arms and legs limp, the men stood over it, studying it.

"Damn thing put up one hell of a fight," Butch said, out of breath.

Ralph looked up at Clive. "What now?"

"We have to destroy its brain or heart. If we don't, this thing could wake up at any moment and kill all of us. I'll grab one arm, and Ralph, you grab the other in case it wakes back up. Butch, you know what to do, right?"

"Yes."

Ralph grabbed the other arm of the beast, pinning it down. Butch removed his hunting knife from his belt and drove it deep into the beast's chest. He did this multiple times before reaching his hand into the monster's chest. Ralph looked away, fighting the urge to vomit at the grotesque sight. Butch slipped his hand into the stab wound and pried open the beast's chest, revealing its heart. Butch then removed the bandana around his neck and used it to safely grip the knife's blade. He then drove the silver handle of the knife into the soft tissue of the beast's heart, killing it once and for all.

The monster let out one last jolt with its limbs, causing Butch to panic and drive the handle into its heart a couple more times. Clive and Ralph fell back in exhaustion but got back up quickly, knowing that time was of the essence. They stood over the deceased beast, whose eyes remained open.

"Kinda ironic that to kill a heartless creature like this, you need to destroy its heart," Ralph noted.

Clive stared at the monster and asked, "Who do you think it was?"

"Honestly, could have been anyone."

"But did you hear Bonnie? She said she was sorry and she should have protected whoever that was. Surely, she knew it was her brother, right?"

Ralph wondered and replied, "It's possible because she was face-to-face with the monster and could look into its eyes. Some say the eyes are the gateway to the soul, and the connection between siblings is only rivaled by the bond between a parent and their child. So, it's possible she stared into the eyes of the monster and saw her brother screaming back at her. More likely, the guilt over what happened to her brother, combined with the immediate threat, made her want to believe it was him. What I do know is that her sacrifice will not go wasted."

Butch pulled the knife from the monster's chest and used the bandana to clean it off. He asked the other two to step back before Clive asked, "Are you sure you know how to do this?"

"I have been working as a farmhand for many years and have skinned my fair share of animals. I mean, nothing to this caliber, but I think I can handle it."

Butch then used his hunting knife to skin the beast. He cut off its pelt before having the other two drape it over him. He volunteered to wear the monster's skin because his stature and frame best fill it out.

"Won't they smell that he's not one of them if they get too close?"

Butch looked at Ralph as if offended by the question. "The skin and blood still attached to the pelt will overpower anything underneath."

"Remember, all you have to do is keep your head down and avoid drawing attention to yourself. You just have to make your way around the saloon and cross the tracks to the jail. There, you will open the sheriff's desk drawer and grab the silver bullets. Then make your way back to safety. As soon as you leave, we will lock the doors and won't open them until you return and state your name. Understood?"

"Yes, sir."

Clive and Ralph unlocked the door and opened it, sending Butch out to what many would consider certain death. Butch walked out into the nightmare with only one thing on his mind: getting the silver bullets. He got on all fours and proceeded to walk like a wolf. He made it past a few of them without a problem, only raising his head to see which direction he was going.

As he approached the jail, Butch came up on a set of paws that stood in his way. It was obvious to him what it was, and he didn't want to risk lifting his head to confirm. He stood stock-still and often had to remind himself to breathe. The werewolf circled him, sniffing what seemed like every inch of the pelt, flashing its razor-sharp teeth as if saying, "I'm on to you." Butch couldn't tell if the amount of sweat pouring off his body was due to the hot July night or the severity of the situation. He also couldn't tell if his shaking was from the monster nudging him with its nose or the pure terror running through his body. Just as the beast started to raise the pelt with its snout, a gunshot rang out in the distance, diverting the monster's attention.

It was one of the remaining locals who stood on his roof, shooting his rifle at the beasts in the street. He must have been watching the three of them from between the two-by-fours that boarded up the windows of his house.

"Come and get it, you bastards!" he yelled. This was very fortunate for Butch, who was able to make it the rest of the way to the jail, but extremely unfortunate for the young man atop his house. He was unaware that his bullets might hurt the beasts, but would ultimately only enrage them.

Butch shut the jail door most of the way, leaving it open just a crack so he could see the outcome of the man's attempt to kill the werewolves. The shooting lasted only a few more seconds before one of the wolves scaled the side of the man's house, reaching the roof. The man frantically continued to shoot the beast before he was lifted high into the air and torn completely in two. Butch looked away from the gruesome scene.

While grateful for the man's help, Butch knew he didn't have time to mourn. He continued toward the sheriff's desk, bumping into a few objects along the way due to the darkness. He fumbled over to the desk and grabbed the six silver revolver rounds that rolled around in the drawer. He emptied the last remaining two lead bullets from his revolver and replaced them with a full cylinder of silver bullets.

He looked outside the window and saw that the beasts were still distracted by their midnight snack on the roof. Butch repositioned the pelt over his body and proceeded back to the storm cellar.

This time, crawling much faster, Butch made it to the tracks in half the time it had taken him before. Butch, in more of a hurry, became sloppy. As he passed the tracks, the pelt caught on a railroad spike, and as he continued forward, it tore loose, remaining attached to the spike. He tried furiously to free the pelt before the beasts noticed, but he heard the footsteps of one approaching.

The beast was twice the size of the others, confirming it was Daniel. The monster, formerly known as Daniel, let out a deafening howl to alert the other beasts. He could have attacked and killed Butch right then, but he wanted to play with his food first. Even as a werewolf, he needed to be a bigger threat than the rest.

Butch took off running, knowing that if he ran back to the storm cellar, Ralph and Clive would be dead for sure. He ran as fast as he could, and while doing so, turned back and fired a silver bullet into the crowd of beasts, hitting one squarely in the forehead. The monster toppled a few times due to the force of the shot, but died on the spot.

Butch made his way to the saloon and ran to the storage room. He slammed the door behind him and locked it as the beasts pounded on it, trying to break in. He was safe for now, or so he thought.

Butch was spent from all the running and sank onto a case of whisky. Unable to see anything, he reached into his back pocket and grabbed one of the matches he kept on him. He struck the match, and it illuminated only a few inches in front of him. Behind him, a shadowy figure moved quickly and ducked behind a stack of boxes. Butch turned to see what it was, but the wind from the movement snuffed out the match. He reached into his back pocket, grabbed another one, and struck it on his boot. Again, it allowed visibility of only a few inches, but he raised his revolver and headed toward the boxes. He got so close that he could see the boxes were labeled. "Fr-a-gile," Butch sounded out, never having been much of a reader.

He tried again to read it, but before he had the chance, a monster lunged out from behind them, knocking Butch over and causing him to drop his gun while the match went out. Butch scrambled back to his feet, blindly swinging at the air, barely able to see an inch in front of his face. The beast swiped at him with its claws, cutting his leg. Butch threw a punch that connected, knocking the werewolf to the ground. He felt around blindly on the ground for his revolver, but couldn't find it. The beast sprang back to its feet and jumped on Butch. He hit and kicked as much as he could, but it didn't seem to matter.

The monster pressed its nose to his, letting out a final roar before Butch, in a last-ditch effort, shoved his hands into its mouth, one hand gripping the roof of its mouth, the other holding its lower jaw. The beast tried to fight free, but Butch's strength was too much. He forced himself to his feet and pulled his hands in opposite directions with all his might, opening the creature's mouth wider. The vicious growl from the animal-like creature turned into a yelp as Butch gave it one last push, ripping the beast's jaw off. He could feel the monster stop moving, signaling it was safe to search for his gun. He lit his last match and found his revolver. Just before the match burned out, he walked over to the beast and shot it once with a silver bullet to ensure it was dead.

Chapter 17

The Search Party

Ralph paced back and forth as Clive sat, watching him. "He's been gone for way too long. It should have taken fifteen, maybe thirty minutes tops, and he's been gone for what seems like double that."

"I think it's best if we stay here. What if he comes back and we're gone?"

"What if we stay here and he doesn't come back?" Ralph interjected.

"Shit, alright! First things first, we can't just go out there like there aren't those things wandering around everywhere. The plan is that we stick together and remain silent. The longer we stay out there, the more likely we are to be killed, so we will canvass the jail and come back if there is no sign of him, even if that means accepting the harsh reality that he is gone. Got it?"

Ralph shook his head.

"How many more rounds do you have? They may not kill those monsters, but they will definitely slow them down."

"About four, and a couple loose in my coat pocket."

"Okay then, let's go find Butch."

Ralph unlocked the chain on the doors, and the two slowly stepped out toward what seemed like certain doom. As they rounded the saloon, two massive beasts waited for them on the other side. Fortunately for Ralph and Clive, they were not spotted, so they quickly hugged the wall to reach the back of the saloon. Ralph looked at Clive as if asking, "What do we do now?"

Clive thought for a moment before loading his revolver and pulling out two bullets. He threw one at a nearby wagon. The bullet hit the wagon with a slight yet noticeable *clink*. The werewolves turned their heads, showing that they had heard the noise, but didn't investigate right away. Clive took the second bullet and threw it at the same wagon, making the same sound, which was enough to lure the beasts over. As the monsters passed them, Ralph and Clive stuck close to the wall to avoid detection.

Once the werewolves passed, they made sure the coast was clear before moving. They hurried to the train tracks, where the pelt that Butch had been wearing lay abandoned. The two glanced at each other with concern, knowing this wasn't a good sign. They also knew they couldn't linger, they were sitting ducks out in the open. Clive grabbed the pelt, and they continued their way to the jail.

Once inside the jail, Ralph made sure to shut the door behind them carefully to ensure that none of the werewolves heard them. Clive rushed to Daniel's desk, but came to the unfortunate discovery of an empty drawer. "Shit," he whispered.

"What?" Ralph replied.

"The silver bullets are gone."

"That's a good thing. That means he has them."

"No. It would be a good thing if he had them and was here with us. This means if he made it out with the gun and was attacked, then they could be anywhere."

"Or this means he's still alive and has one of the only surefire ways to kill these bastards. He has to be somewhere else."

"Okay, say he is still alive and hiding somewhere else, where would he have run to?"

Ralph thought for a moment before blurting out, "The saloon!"

"What?" Clive responded.

"The saloon."

"Those double-swinging doors can barely be locked, let alone keep a monster out. He'd be just as likely to be eaten alive in there as he would outside."

"Yes, but not in the back storage room, the same room where we hid you from Daniel. The only problem is the door won't hold very long with one or more of those things beating on it."

"What do you suggest we do?" Clive asked.

"The only thing to do. We've got to go after him."

"We can't both just walk out there looking for him. We'd be dead for sure."

Clive looked down at the pelt he had in his hand and said, "But we can go out there undetected."

Ralph took the pelt from Clive's hand and said, "Great. I'll go and look for him."

"Whoa, whoa, whoa, slow down there. I think it would be best if I go out there instead of you."

"Why's that?" Ralph asked.

"Well, for starters, I reckon I've killed more of those things than you."

"I reckon I didn't realize we were in a pissing contest and not very long ago, you wanted to stay in the storm cellar until morning."

"Yes, but we are here now, and it's way too late to turn back. Besides, I owe you guys for saving my skin earlier."

Clive took the pelt from Ralph and threw it over himself, while Ralph stood behind him, making sure it looked convincing from the back. He turned to Ralph, who gave him a thumbs-up, and Clive headed out the door.

He slowly made his way towards the saloon, passing a few beasts along the way. He passed the double-swinging doors and took a moment to remove a couple of pieces of gravel that had embedded in his hands from crawling on his hands and knees. After removing the gravel, he continued to the back of the saloon.

He didn't make it too far before coming to a crowd of werewolves, growling and periodically attacking the door. Off to the side, like a general commanding his army, stood the massive beast formerly known as Daniel. It seemed he couldn't be bothered with the dirty work of opening the door, but he would be the first to claim the prize behind it.

Knowing that Butch had to be behind that door, Clive did his best to slip out from the crowd without being noticed and made his way back to the jail.

Clive successfully made it back to the jail and knocked on the door quietly so as not to be detected by the monsters. By the sound of the knock, Ralph knew it was Clive because it sounded like knuckles on wood, not a hair-covered paw. Just to be safe, he opened the door ever so slightly to peek through the crack first. After confirming it was Clive, he opened the door the rest of the way.

"Well, where is Butch? Don't tell me they got him," Ralph asked, desperation in his voice.

Clive removed the pelt from over his head. "I can't say for sure, but there is definitely something behind that door that has their attention."

Ralph smirked. "That's good news, that means he is still alive."

"Well, the bad news is that the door separating him from at least four of those very angry things doesn't look like it will hold much longer. So, we need an idea, and we need one fast."

The two thought for a moment.

"Tell me, where can I find the nearest barn?" Clive asked.

"I mean, there used to be a slew of ranchers and farmers that settled down here before this whole nightmare rolled into town. After Daniel's crusade for revenge, most of them were either driven out of business because their cattle were killed by those monsters, attacked and turned into those monsters themselves, or simply disappeared. I usually buy meat for the saloon from Jeb Surely. His barn is about five minutes south, but it is very well fortified due to those things roaming around. Why?"

"Are you in good standing with Jeb?"

"I'd say so, given that selling to the saloon is his biggest source of revenue."

"I think we should pay Mr. Surely a visit."

"Okay, but how are we going to get out of here without being noticed by those monsters? We only have one of those pelts."

Clive continued to think, searching for an answer to the glaring hole in his plan. He handed the pelt to Ralph.

"What's this?" Ralph asked.

"Well, you have a rapport with this Jeb fellow, so what better person to go and ask him for help?"

"What about you?"

"We only have one of those pelts, so we both can't safely go. Remember to keep your head down and avoid drawing any attention to yourself."

Ralph was hesitant but eventually agreed, putting the plan into motion. He knew time was of the essence. He exited the jail wearing the pelt and began to walk quickly south. He knew that not all of the beasts were trying to get into the saloon's storage room, so if he came across one, he would have to stop and drop to all fours to hide his face. Surprisingly, he made it to Jeb's farm without any issues.

Ralph pounded on Jeb's house doors to no answer. Jeb was either asleep or smart enough not to answer the door while monsters roamed the street. Ralph turned to the barn and ran to it. He tried to open the doors, but they were chained and locked. He tugged on the chains as hard as he could, to no avail. Suddenly, he heard a loud *bang*, followed by a sharp pain in his leg. He screamed as loud as he could, knowing it wasn't smart, but the pain was too intense. A man ran over with his gun pointed at Ralph.

"I got you, you son of a bitch. You think I'm just gonna hide inside while you eat away my livelihood?" the man said.

The man, still thinking he had shot a monster, stood over Ralph and cocked his gun.

"Wait, stop!" Ralph screamed.

"What? Those beasts can't talk."

"That's because it's me, Ralph, you damn fool. You shot me in my leg."

"Oh my, Ralph, I didn't know it was you. Why are you dressed up as one of those monsters?"

Ralph, trying to fight the pain and stay as quiet as possible, said, "I don't have much time to explain, but we need to get inside in case one of those things heard the gunshot."

Jeb helped Ralph to his feet and did his best to hold him up as he guided him into the house. Inside, Ralph sat in a chair while Jeb used a match to light a lamp. Jeb left the room and came back with a bottle of whisky, a couple of towels, and a handkerchief.

"All right, let's take a look at that leg. I have to clean it and wrap this around it to hopefully stop the bleeding."

Ralph lifted his leg and rolled up his pant leg. The bullet had entered through his right calf and exited through the front of his leg. The wound was bleeding quite a bit, but at least it wasn't fatal.

Jeb handed Ralph a towel and said, "You might want to bite down on this."

Ralph put the towel in his mouth as Jeb poured the whisky onto the wound. Ralph grimaced from a pain so strong that he could feel it everywhere from his leg to his teeth. Jeb used the towels to press down on the wound to stop the bleeding, and as it slowed, he tied the handkerchief around Ralph's leg. Jeb stood up, grabbed another chair, and sat down in front of him.

"Now, you want to tell me why in the hell you were trying to break into my barn dressed as one of those things? I could have shot you dead, and I'd be digging a hole in the morning for you instead of just fixing up your leg."

"Luckily for me, you could never hit the broad side of a barn," Ralph said with a half smirk, the pain still etched across his face.

"Mock me all you want, but it's because of my piss-poor aim that you're still breathing."

Ralph looked at Jeb with a straight face. "We started a fight that I'm starting to doubt we can even win."

"What do you mean?" Jeb asked.

"Well, remember that group of outlaws that shot up the hanging earlier?"

"Oh no, that was you?"

"Well, me and a couple of my friends."

"But why?"

"What do you mean, why? Aren't you tired of living in fear? Living in a world where monsters roam the streets and the people we look to for protection are even scarier than them?"

"I mean, I understand things aren't ideal around here at the moment, but the sheriff says there are better days ahead. This is just a minor setback on the way to greater prosperity."

"That's all nonsense he's been feeding everyone in order to keep them in line. Besides, now he's revealed his true form, he's become one of those things. That's why we need to finish this tonight, because come tomorrow, he'll be looking for Butch, Clive, and me. That's where you come in. You see, I need to take some of your livestock into town as a distraction."

"But my livestock is my livelihood. Without them, I can't stay in business."

"Don't you see this is much bigger than your business!" Ralph yelled, becoming impatient.

Jeb got up and walked out of the room, looking visibly upset. Ralph remained seated, staring ahead and trying not to move his leg while he continued to plead his case.

"Listen, Jeb, if money is what you're worried about, the saloon is more than happy to pay you for it tomorrow when everything is said and done, but for now, my friends are in trouble."

That was when Ralph felt something sharp press into his back.

"Jeb?" he said, his voice slightly cracking.

Jeb held a knife against Ralph's back, and in his other hand, he held two pieces of rope.

"I liked you, Ralph, which really makes me wish you hadn't told me any of that. Not only did you try to kill Sheriff Freeman this morning, but you also want me to be an accomplice by using my livelihood to help take him down. Don't even try to reach for your gun, I can slit your throat before you even have a chance to lay your hand on the handle."

Jeb now moved the knife from Ralph's back to his neck. The cold metal bit into Ralph's skin, giving him goosebumps.

"Now listen, Jeb, you and I both know Daniel isn't the real Sheriff Freeman," Ralph said.

Jeb snapped, "You talk about him as if he's gone. If what you say is true, he'll turn back tomorrow and bring you and your delinquent friends to justice. I can't believe you decided to save a murderer like Clive Holiday and turn your back on this town, your home."

Ralph began to sweat even more.

"You and I both know this isn't the same place we moved to way back when. I don't even recognize what it's become. You can't stand there and tell me you've bought into the lies Daniel's been feeding us."

"You're lying. Sheriff Freeman warned us about people like you—you and that murderer you saved this morning. You know he killed Doctor Kelp in cold blood, right? Burned him and his wife alive. Now he's running free when he should be burning in hell himself."

Ralph closed his eyes and tried to swallow the lump in his throat. "Daniel lied to you. He just wanted to kill Clive because he knew the truth. As for the doctor, it was all a misunderstanding."

"Misunderstanding? He took Paul and his lovely wife's life. Instead of owning up to what he did, he ran like a coward. That is the kind of man you willingly tied yourself to."

"So, what now? Are you going to slit my throat here and have me bleed out on the floor?"

"No, sir. I don't believe a yellow-bellied traitor such as yourself deserves such a quick punishment. I am going to tie you up and bring you into town first thing in the morning on my horse's back. I'll turn you over to the sheriff. He'll probably make a public example of you to lure your friends out. Now, I'm going to need you to stay still while I tie your hands and legs, or a hole in your leg will be the least of your problems. First, slowly remove the revolver from your hip."

Ralph slowly removed the revolver from his holster and placed it on the table beside him. Jeb grabbed the revolver and tucked it into the waistband of his pants. He then removed the knife from Ralph's throat and, slowly and lightly, pressed it between his shoulder blades and down his back. Then he continued tying Ralph's legs.

Ralph noticed that Jeb had to set down the knife to use both hands to tie his limbs. As Jeb bent down to tie his legs,

Ralph took the opportunity to kick backward, his boot connecting squarely with Jeb's nose. The impact broke Jeb's nose and knocked him back. Ralph gritted his teeth from the pressure he had to put on his injured leg. Before Jeb could get up, Ralph lunged forward and pinned him down. Jeb, his face now a bloody mess, didn't go down without a fight.

Ralph threw another punch, landing square on Jeb's already-broken nose. If it wasn't broken before, it certainly was now. Ralph pushed himself up to grab the knife lying behind him, but Jeb reached out and clutched his former friend's injured leg. He ripped off the handkerchief and jammed his thumb into the bullet hole, causing Ralph to scream and collapse to the floor.

Jeb snatched up the knife and straddled Ralph. He raised it high and brought it down with all his strength. Ralph thrust his hand upward, blocking the blade before it could make contact. They struggled, the knife inching closer to Ralph's throat. That was when Ralph shot his right hand up and seized Jeb by his shattered, bloody nose. Jeb screamed and fell back as the struggle raged on.

Ralph crawled on top of Jeb and wrapped his hands around his throat, squeezing with all his strength. He pressed down harder, thinking the struggle might finally be over, until a sharp, piercing pain shot through his side. He looked down and saw that Jeb had stabbed him in the right side. Still, Ralph didn't stop. He kept tightening his grip until the same searing pain struck again.

He released the pressure on Jeb's throat just as Jeb lifted the knife again. Ralph lunged forward, grabbing Jeb's wrist and the hand holding the knife, then sank his teeth into him. Jeb screamed in agony and dropped the knife. Ralph snatched it up, raised it high above his head, and drove it down with all his strength, the blade slicing clean through Jeb's hand and into the wooden floor beneath.

Jeb was now pinned to the ground, and Ralph took the chance to pummel him with several more punches until Jeb fell unconscious.

Breathing heavily, Ralph lifted his blood-soaked shirt, revealing two deep puncture wounds in his side. He collapsed backward, drained from exhaustion and blood loss. As he lay there, his thoughts began to drift. He wondered if any of this had been worth it or if he had only been blinded by the false hope of making this once-great town safe again. He imagined a place where he might someday meet a kind woman and raise a family of his own. A tear slid down his cheek as that dream slipped further away and the darkness began to close in. Moments later, Ralph lost consciousness.

About thirty minutes passed before Ralph regained consciousness. He was weak from blood loss, but managed to push himself to his feet. He limped over to the rope Jeb had dropped and grabbed one of the strands, tying Jeb's legs together with slow, shaky hands. Then he limped back to grab the other strand of rope and returned to Jeb, who still wasn't moving.

Ralph fell to his knees, gripped the knife handle, and wrenched it free from the floor and Jeb's hand. He then tied Jeb's wrists together and reached into the waistband of the unconscious man's pants to retrieve the gun.

Ralph slowly made his way outside in search of a stable. He found one opposite the barn, but like the barn, it was locked. Ralph cocked the revolver and fired at the padlock. The first shot damaged it, but it remained intact. He fired again, this time blowing the lock apart. Inside was Jeb's horse, snorting and stomping in panic from the loud gunfire.

Ralph tried his best to calm the animal, whispering softly as he led it toward the front of the house. His bloody handprints streaked across its white coat, staining the mane a dark red. He staggered back into the house and, with every ounce of strength left in him, heaved the hog-tied captive onto his shoulder. The effort tore a scream from his throat, and he collapsed to the floor, gasping in pain.

After lying there for a moment, Ralph pushed himself up again. This time, with gritted teeth and trembling arms, he managed to carry Jeb outside and hoist him onto the back of the horse. Ralph mounted behind him, barely able to stay upright, and spurred the horse forward toward town.

About fifty feet from the center of town, Ralph could see the shadows of the beasts in the distance. He slowly dismounted the horse and removed Jeb's body from the back. He put the hog-tied Jeb on the ground and groggily walked to the horse's head. He kissed it and said, "Good girl," before slapping it on the hindquarters, causing the horse to run into town. The horse ran past the beasts, getting their attention, and the monsters chased it through town. With the coast clear, Ralph was able to drag Jeb, who was now coming to, into town.

Back at the jail, Clive heard a knock on the door. "Took you long enough," he said as he opened it. As he slowly opened the door, he saw Ralph, white as a ghost, collapse in the doorway. "What the hell?" Clive said, pulling him and the now-conscious Jeb into the jail. Ralph once again passed out.

Clinging to life, Ralph came to, sitting propped up against one of the jail cells. "Clive," he barely got out. Clive rushed to him and asked what was going on.

"H-H-He attacked me. I couldn't get the livestock, but thought we could use him for the plan," Ralph said as he coughed.

Clive turned to Jeb.

"Untie me, you murdering son of a bitch! Once tomorrow comes, justice will be served! You will hang for this, you hear me, you will hang!"

Clive walked over to him, weeping, and took his gun out. He pressed it against the side of Jeb's head and yelled for him to shut his mouth. "Don't," Ralph barely whispered. Clive, knowing that Butch's life depended on this plan working, put his gun into his holster and peeked outside.

"What about those things outside? If I drag him out there, they will attack me for sure," Clive said.

"I set the horse free, and the ones nearby chased it. Depending on whether they caught it or not, you should have a small window of opportunity. So you are going to have to act now and act fast."

Clive walked over to Ralph, knelt beside him, and whispered, "You are going to be fine."

"No, he's not," Jeb laughed.

On the verge of death, Ralph reached into his pocket and pulled out the knife he had taken from Jeb's house, and gave Clive a nod. Clive took it and tucked it into his back pocket as if he knew what to do with it. He then picked up Jeb and threw him over his shoulder, carrying him outside. He proceeded to move slowly but efficiently across the train tracks toward the storm cellar. He threw Jeb to the ground, who landed with a thud, and opened both doors. He lifted the infuriated Jeb back up and carried him into the back of the cellar. Clive placed him down and stared at Jeb for a moment. A bloody Jeb stared back before spitting a bloody loogie in Clive's face. Clive smirked, took the knife from his back pocket, and cut the restraints from Jeb's legs and hands. Jeb could try to fight Clive, but knew he didn't stand a chance against someone armed.

"I will be out of here in the morning, you know that, right?" Jeb said.

Clive didn't say anything as he left, taking two of the kerosene lamps from the wall with him. He then headed toward the saloon, where the four beasts were still trying to get into the storage room, but he noticed that the hulking Daniel was no longer there. Clive raised his gun in the air and fired. *BANG!* The four beasts turned toward Clive. They all bared their teeth and started running after him. Clive sprinted as fast as he could around the saloon to the back. When the beasts arrived, Clive was nowhere to be found.

The beasts searched around the back for a moment but found nothing. As they stood there, faint shouts echoed from the storm cellar. The monsters growled as they approached the cellar doors. They ripped them from their hinges and slowly crept into the dimly lit underground room.

Down there wasn't Clive but Jeb, whose shouts of rage turned into screams of terror as the four beasts lunged toward him. Hearing the screams, Clive rounded the corner of the saloon with the two kerosene lamps and hurled them into the storm cellar. The lamps crashed, one striking a werewolf and setting it ablaze, while the other shattered in front of the beasts, creating a wall of fire.

The monsters howled in panic as they burst out of the cellar, burning. They stumbled and writhed before their charred bodies finally collapsed to the ground, dead. Clive ran back around the building to get Butch.

Chapter 18

Goodbye Fearless Leader

Clive walked over to the storage room door with a lit kerosene lamp, the door beaten down and hanging on for dear life by one hinge. Clive slowly opened it, hoping their efforts hadn't been for nothing. Butch was sitting on a box of whisky, and at his feet lay one of those massive beasts, the bottom half of its jaw just barely hanging on to its face by a single strand of bloody muscle.

"Well, aren't you a sight for sore eyes," Butch said.

"Looks like you were able to hold your own against those bastards pretty well. Please tell me you were able to get your hands on those silver bullets," Clive replied.

Butch handed over his revolver and, in return, Clive handed over his. "There were six bullets, but I had to use one to get myself out of a pinch and the other on this piece of garbage. So, we are down to four, and I am not much for math, but there are a lot more than four of those monsters left roaming around out there."

"Then I guess we are going to have to make every one of these bullets count."

"Where's Ralph? Is he back in the storm cellar?"

Clive hung his head.

"Clive?"

"Well, you see, Ralph went to get some help from a nearby farmer he knew, and the guy turned out to be one of Daniel's followers. It's bad... really bad."

"No, no, no," Butch said, tears welling in his eyes.

"He's back at the jail, but he was barely hanging on when I left to come get you."

Butch rushed past Clive and headed for the jail without any regard for his safety. He burst through the double doors of the saloon, and on the other side stood one of the monsters. It lunged at Butch, and he ducked, causing the beast to fly over him.

BANG! Clive was right behind him and fired a silver bullet at the airborne creature, striking it clean between the eyes. The werewolf hit the ground like a sack of potatoes, dead. Without hesitation, Butch got up and continued toward the jail, Clive hot on his heels.

Butch burst through the jail door, and his heart sank. Propped up against the cell, hunched over on the floor with his eyes shut, was Ralph. His skin was pale, and his shirt was soaked in blood. Blood also poured from a hole in his leg. His breathing was shallow, and his pulse faint.

Butch took a seat next to the barely alive man who, not even a day ago, had dreamed of a world where they no longer had to live in fear. He was a strong man who had seen the horrors this world had to offer and who would have walked through hell if it meant saving the town he loved.

"It's bad, isn't it?" Ralph managed to get out, his eyes barely opening.

"You've never lied to me, so I owe you the same respect. It doesn't look good, my friend."

Clive stood at the doorway, watching the two men.

"I gotta tell ya, Ralph, when you first came to me with this whole plan, a part of me thought you were crazy. After thinking it over, I realized, what better way to fight Daniel's evil than to have someone just as crazy fighting for good and justice?"

"We all have a little bit of that madness in us, it is how we use it that separates us from those monsters out there. Daniel had a chance to use his newfound power for good and to unite us against this evil, but he chose to turn us against one another."

"I wish a guy like you were there to fill the position instead of Daniel."

"I just wish I could finish what we started here, but instead the nightmare goes on," Ralph uttered, blood pooling at the corner of his mouth.

Clive stepped forward.

"Now you listen here, Ralph, Butch and I are still here, and you better believe we will end this tonight. I have made many mistakes in my life and committed sins I can't be forgiven for, so if for some reason, I was put here in this horror to help, then I will fight with every last breath left in my lungs."

Ralph mustered the last of his strength and shot Clive a slight smirk before saying, "You are a good man, Clive Holiday." With that, Ralph's eyes closed and his head dropped. The man who once had a vision was now a mangled vessel for a kind soul barely hanging on.

"Is he gone?" Clive asked.

Butch checked his pulse before saying, "He's unconscious, but he's barely hanging on." Butch grabbed Ralph's feet, Clive seized him by his shoulders, and the two men placed Ralph on the cot in the cell so he would be more comfortable in his final moments on this earth.

Butch kissed Ralph on the forehead and whispered, "Goodbye, our fearless leader."

Clive and Butch walked out of the cell toward the door of the jail.

"Who is the bastard that did this?" Butch demanded.

"Ralph said his name was Jeb Surely."

"Jeb Surely?"

"You know him?"

"Yeah, he was the saloon's biggest supplier for meats and such. They were friends. Why would he do this?" Butch said.

"He bought into Daniel's corrupt vision of the future. Ralph went over to his house to get his help, but instead, Jeb stabbed him multiple times."

"Why are we just standing here, then? Let's go find the son of a bitch and cut him from forehead to belly button." Butch said, pulling his knife from his hip.

"You think Ralph went down without a fight? Even bleeding out like a stuffed pig, he was able to hogtie the coward and bring him all the way back here. We gave Mr. Surely a fitting send-off, fed him to the wolves, if you will."

"Good, I hope he felt every razor-sharp tooth puncture that skin of his," Butch said, putting his knife away.

"At least some justice has been served through all of this. But what now?"

"What do you mean?" Butch asked.

"You've known Ralph a long time and obviously discussed how this would go down."

"I know you're not going to believe me, but I was just the quiet strongman of this operation. He didn't lay out the details, just the big picture of what life would be like after we slay all the beasts. It was honestly all talk at first, more of a bonding thing between him, Jack, Bonnie, and me, but then he caught wind of you, Clive Holiday."

"Me?"

"That's right. Once he heard of a man who'd been on trial for murder whose defense was self-defense from a werewolf, he knew it was someone he needed on his side. Don't you see, Clive, there's nothing random about you being here. You were the final push a good man needed to set change in motion. Whatever you did in your past, good or bad, has led you here to put an end to this. Who knows, when it's all said and done, the man upstairs may look at the good you've done here and still let you in."

"Well, there's one thing you're dead wrong about, Butch."

"Oh yeah? What's that?"

"You are far more than just the strongman of the operation."

Butch grinned. "Alright, we can't just stay here. What are we going to do?" They both took a moment to contemplate their next move. "Say, why were you going to get Jeb's help?"

"Ralph said he had a barn not far from here, and we thought we could use his cattle as a distraction to get to you before it was too late. Worst-case scenario, we'd find another place of refuge if need be since I set the storm cellar on fire."

"I was thinking that since you guys used him as a midnight snack for those monsters, we don't need his permission to use his livestock anymore, but I need you to show me the basement first."

Butch lit a lamp as Clive walked into the cell where Ralph was lying and took the revolver from the unconscious man's waist. He stared at the blood-covered man for a moment.

He thought it odd Ralph hadn't been able to see his mission through to the end, yet he looked at peace. Maybe he was going crazy, but Clive, even if only for a moment, thought Ralph knew that if he wasn't going to make it, he had found two men with as much heart as he to see the plan through. Two men who had more heart than brains and believed what they were doing tonight might actually make a difference in this savage world.

"This is for you, buddy," Clive told Ralph.

Chapter 19

Belly of the Beast

Butch led the way with the lantern down the stairs to the basement. They walked past the cells that used to contain the so-called "prisoners". The stench of stale blood filled the narrow basement, causing Clive to pull his coat collar over his nose. Limbs from Daniel's victims littered the cell floors. "Sick" was the only word Clive could use to describe the whole scene. The two went to the back of the basement and stopped.

"What the…"

Butch was at a loss for words. Amazed, he stared at the mountain of explosives that lay before him.

"What is all of this?" Butch asked, dumbfounded.

"Daniel brought me down here after I was arrested and told me that he needed all of these explosives and gunpowder to expand the basement so he could house more of those creatures."

"With that amount of dynamite, gunpowder, and TNT, he would be able to wipe out a whole town. So, unless he was going to build a castle for those things, who knows what his malicious intentions were."

"Why did you want me to bring you down here?"

"It might be risky, but I think we should transport some of this to that no-good Jeb's barn."

"How much are we talking? It will take well into the morning to bring all of this there, all the while trying not to get eaten by those things."

"I'm going to need you to stuff a few sticks of dynamite into your jacket, and I am strong enough to carry one of those boxes of gunpowder. You can lead the way to Jeb's barn as I direct you. You'll have the silver bullets ready in case you need to put one of those bastards down. Do you think you can do that?"

Clive nodded in agreement.

"Good. Now, when we go back up, we should look in the sheriff's desk for matches because I'm running dangerously low."

Clive grabbed two sticks of dynamite and stuck them in the right side of his coat. He then grabbed two more sticks and stuffed them in the left side. Butch reached down to grab the crate of gunpowder. As he picked it up, the look on his face showed it was a struggle even for the strongman.

"Are you sure you've got it?" Clive asked, noticing the slight struggle.

"Yeah, yeah, I've got it," Butch said. "Just had to get on my feet. Now, if you don't mind picking up that lamp so I can see where I'm going. Don't get too close because if that flame gets near this, then you, me, and this plan will be blown sky-high."

Clive bent down and picked up the lamp, but as he did, one of the sticks of dynamite fell out of his pocket. A gasp from both him and Butch filled the dark basement. If the fuse from the dynamite somehow met with that flame, surrounded by all these explosives, then it'd be game over. Nothing but a crater in the earth would be left of them. Clive looked up and let out an uncomfortable chuckle while Butch remained standing there with his hands full and eyes wide.

"That would've been a fitting end to this nightmare," Clive said with a low chuckle.

Butch gave a smirk and said, "Let's get a move on, we're burning moonlight."

Clive picked up the lantern and led the way upstairs, with Butch trailing close behind. Clive walked to the desk and opened the drawer. Papers littered it, but after a few moments of rummaging, he found a small box of matches. He grabbed them and shoved them deep into his dungaree pocket.

The two took one last look at Ralph, who looked as though death was moments away from claiming him, and then stepped out into the hot July night.

They moved carefully away from the jail, Clive leading the way with the lamp and Butch following close behind, giving directions in a low tone so as not to draw attention.

"It's a straight shot, can't miss it," Butch whispered.

Clive continued forward, but he couldn't shake the feeling that they were being watched, stalked like prey by a hunter, except this time, the prey was hunting them. Off in the distance, cactuses took the shape of beasts, forcing him to glance twice before realizing his mistake. The quiet night air was the most unsettling part, because they both knew the monsters were out there waiting.

Oddly enough, they made it to Jeb's barn without incident. Maybe their luck was turning around, or maybe the werewolves were just playing with their food.

"Alright, we're here," Butch said, setting the crate of gunpowder down gently.

He walked over to the barn door, where a large lock barred their way inside.

"Do we break into his house and search for the key?" Clive asked.

"Not unless you know where he hid it. For all we know, it could've been on him when the werewolves got to him."

Thump… Thump…

"What was that?" Clive asked, his voice wary.

"I think we may have company. You stay here with the gunpowder, and I'll go check it out. First, give me the revolver with the silver bullets."

"Wait, then how am I supposed to defend myself?"

"You've got four sticks of dynamite in your jacket. I'm sure you'll be just fine."

Clive handed Butch the revolver. Butch moved silently along the side of the barn, careful to mask the sound of his footsteps. As he rounded the corner, he froze. There it was.

The creature was sniffing the dirt, tracking their scent. Its back was turned to Butch, giving him the upper hand.

He crept closer, muscles tight, then lunged his left arm, locking around the beast's neck from behind.

The werewolf thrashed violently, claws raking the air, but Butch's strength held firm.

With his right hand, he raised the revolver to the creature's head. *BANG!*

The silver bullet tore through one side of its skull and exited clean out the other.

The werewolf went from writhing fury to dead weight in an instant.

Butch took a deep breath, steadied himself, and began heading back toward the front of the barn. "I assume you took care of one of those damn monsters," Clive said as he noticed Butch walking back.

"I'm getting tired of this shit."

Without hesitation, Butch pointed the revolver at the padlock on the door and pulled the trigger. *BANG!* The lock fell to the ground in two pieces, and the men were now able to access the barn.

"What are you doing?" Clive yelled.

"What do you mean? I got us into the barn."

"Okay, but is that the revolver I just gave you?"

"Yeah, why?"

"It was the gun containing the silver bullets, you fool. You just wasted one of our only surefire ways to kill these bastards. How many do we have left?"

Butch opened the chamber of the gun. "One," he uttered, disappointed in himself.

"Not to be a jerk, but there are a lot more than one of those things ready to kill us out there. What do we do now?"

Clive took the revolver with the special bullets back from Butch and holstered it.

"First things first, we get into the barn, because who knows how many of them are on their way to investigate the gunshots. We're nothin' but sitting ducks out here just asking to be eaten."

Butch walked over to the crate of gunpowder and lifted it up as Clive opened the barn doors. Inside were the usual suspects: cows, sheep, and pigs. Butch safely made it into the barn with the gunpowder, and as Clive was closing the barn doors behind him, one of the beasts grabbed him and swept him away.

The beast had Clive under its arm, carrying him into the night. He tried kicking and biting the monster to no effect. He reached for the revolver that contained the silver bullets, but couldn't get a firm grip on it. Clive knew the longer he remained in the monster's grasp, the further away he'd be taken from the barn; therefore, he knew he needed to act quickly. In an act of desperation, he reached into his jacket pocket and grabbed a stick of dynamite. With all his might, he began jabbing it at the beast. As Clive yelled in distress, he was able to drive his arm up with great force, jamming the stick of dynamite into the monster's eye socket. The monster roared in pain and released its grip on Clive. Clive knew that there was only one way now to kill the beast.

After a moment of hesitation, Clive reached into his pocket and pulled out a match. Still shaken by the horror before him, he managed to gather his wits and struck the match on his boot. He walked up to the flailing monster, igniting the fuse and dodging the blind beast's wild swipes before running in the opposite direction toward the barn. He got a safe enough distance away before he heard a final, piercing howl followed by a thunderous explosion.

As he was running back to the barn, a flaming, dismembered arm from the monster landed right in front of him. "Oh, shit!" he said to himself.

Clive made his way back to the barn and banged on the doors. "Butch, open up!" he yelled. After a moment, still, nobody answered, "What are you trying to do, Butch? Get me killed? Open up!"

The barn doors opened, revealing a shaken Butch.

"Clive? Is that you? I thought you were a goner for sure. Quick, get in here before something else happens to you."

Without saying another word, Clive entered the barn, and Butch closed the door securely behind him. Clive fell back onto a pile of hay and shut his eyes, his chest rising and falling with heavy breaths. Butch stood there, staring at the clearly exhausted and hurt man.

"Well, how did you get back?"

"What do you mean? I walked. What kind of question is that?"

"Alright, smartass, you know what I mean. How did you get out of the clutches of that beast? Did you end up using the last silver bullet?"

Without opening his eyes, Clive reached into his coat's inner pocket and pulled out a stick of dynamite. He opened his eyes ever so slightly and said, "One of these bad boys," before giving it a kiss.

"Wait, what?"

"What are you not understanding, Butch? I blew it up. Nothing left of that werewolf but a couple of limbs, a hole in the ground, and the stench of burnt fur."

Butch stood there, rather impressed by Clive's quick thinking, before an idea came to him that anyone would think made him mad. He hurried over to the cattle and began to sprinkle gunpowder over them.

"What are you doing?" Clive asked, turning to him.

There was no answer from Butch as he continued to dust the cattle with gunpowder. Clive stood up, clearly annoyed that Butch was wasting the valuable resources.

"Hey, I asked what you're doing."

Clive walked over to Butch and grabbed his hand that held a fistful of gunpowder.

"Are you a madman?"

Without breaking eye contact, Butch smirked and said, "I might be mad, but if this works, we can take out a whole slew of those flesh-eating creatures without having to use that last silver bullet."

"What do you mean?" Clive asked.

"Just trust me," Butch said before yanking his hand free.

Clive continued to watch Butch frantically douse the cattle in gunpowder before he was asked to open the doors. Clive was hesitant to do so. Where they were was relatively safe, but he needed to trust Butch's instinct. Like it or not, there's a certain bond that forms when you've fought werewolves alongside someone.

Clive let out a final sigh before opening the door. Butch led a pig outside and then ran back in. The pig wandered around for a couple of minutes, oinking, before two beasts suddenly leapt from the shadows and attacked.

The monsters tore the pig's flesh from its bones and devoured the meat in seconds. When they finished, the creatures turned toward the barn and charged straight at the two men.

Butch and Clive both drew their revolvers and pulled the triggers. *BANG!* The bullets seemed to travel in slow motion before hitting the werewolves. *BOOM!* In a violent explosion of red and pink mist, the beasts were obliterated.

"What the—" was all Clive could say before Butch grabbed him by his coat collar and dragged him back into the barn, slamming the door shut behind them. "What the hell just happened? Those beasts just exploded."

"Simple, my friend. I poured gunpowder on the cattle, gunpowder being very combustible. The monsters took the bait, and there you have it. Can't believe it actually worked."

"So, what now?"

"Now we open the door and release all the cattle into the seemingly peaceful night, hoping they lure out more of those monsters. After that, it's just target practice for us."

"Yeah, if the target's moving fast, strong as hell, and has an insatiable appetite for flesh."

Butch chuckled and told Clive they'd best get moving, dawn wasn't far off. Clive went to the door and opened it while Butch wrangled the rest of the cattle outside. Cows, pigs, and sheep gathered nervously just beyond the barn doors, their low moans echoing in the tense night air.

"Come on! Get!" Butch yelled.

The cattle didn't move.

"They can't stay here, it's like we're inviting the werewolves right inside the barn."

Butch grabbed his revolver and fired into the sky. *BANG!* The shot startled the animals, sending them stampeding into the night. It didn't take long before the monsters descended upon the gunpowder-covered prey. The sound of at least six beasts attacking and feeding at once was the stuff of nightmares. The quiet July night was filled with the disturbing squeals of pigs and the desperate mooing of cows, as if they were begging the wolves for mercy.

For a brief moment, Clive's eyes welled with tears. These poor, defenseless animals were just pawns in their desperate plan. You'd think a meat-eater like him would understand it was simply the cruel law of survival.

When the slaughter was nearly done, Butch and Clive raised their revolvers, aiming at the feasting beasts.

"Now!" Butch shouted.

BANG! BANG! The gunfire echoed throughout the town. The bullets ripped through the air, striking one monster in the leg and another in the shoulder. However, the shots had little effect. The beasts turned toward them, their wolf-like eyes glowing with rage, locking onto the two men like predators ready to pounce.

"Oh hell! Why didn't it do anything?" Clive shouted. "I don't know! It should've worked! You saw it yourself!"

The two fired another round at the charging beasts. Just like before, the bullets tore from the barrels and, in the blink of an eye, slammed into the monsters' flesh, this time hitting them in the stomach.

BOOM! BOOM!

In less than a second, the beasts went from snarling fury to an explosion of limbs and entrails, the blast shaking the ground only a few feet away.

"That's it! Aim for their stomachs!" Butch yelled.

Within moments, the remaining four monsters were reduced to nothing more than smears of blood and shredded flesh on the dirt. The moon hung high in the sky, casting a pale, ghostly light over the carnage, enough to make any sane man's stomach turn.

Bones from the slaughtered cattle littered the ground, and if they listened closely, they could swear they still heard the faint, haunting cries of the dying animals echoing in the warm night air. The two men stood in silence, not to admire their handiwork, but in disbelief that this nightmare was real. Only a week ago, Clive had been robbing travelers for a few dollars. Folks would've called him a lowlife, but now here he was, fighting to save a town from creatures straight out of a nightmare.

Butch, on the other hand, understood the situation better. He had been here from the beginning. He'd watched friends and loved ones either get devoured or turned into one of those beasts. A man who had once led a simple life as a farmhand was now unofficially tasked with saving his town. A man who once sat in the saloon with his buddies, dreaming of a day they could live without fear, had now, within a single night, seen every one of those friends slaughtered.

"Alright, let's get back into the barn before more of those things show up," Clive said.

The two headed back into the barn and shut the door behind them. They sat down on the ground for a moment, trying to catch their breath, when they heard rustling to their left, behind a bale of hay.

At first, they brushed it off, thinking it was a pig they'd forgotten to round up, but then they noticed the breathing. It was heavier, rougher, and not like any normal animal.

Their safe haven might now be the most dangerous place on earth.

Chapter 20

We Can't Stay Here

Before the two had a moment to react, the monster lunged from behind the bales of hay, knocking them both to the ground. Clive pulled out the revolver containing the silver bullet, but before he could fire, the creature swiped it from his hand, sending it flying into one of the pens.

Butch sprang into action, charging shoulder-first into the beast and knocking it back. The monster roared, growing more enraged by the second. Butch grabbed its arm, but the werewolf's strength was overwhelming. It slammed its arm, with Butch still clinging to it, against a support beam, knocking him out cold.

The beast then turned its attention to Clive and charged. Clive spun around and ran toward the door, fumbling with the latch as he tried to open it. He glanced back. The creature was stalking him slowly now, its movements deliberate, almost playful. It was as if the monster was mocking him, knowing full well that Clive had nowhere left to run.

Clive slid to the ground with his back against the door, raising his trembling hands in a desperate plea.

"Please, no," he whispered. The monster leaned in until its snout was inches from Clive's face, baring its jagged teeth. The seemingly defenseless man shut his eyes tight, praying for a miracle.

The monster howled, ready to bring this night to an end. As it lifted its head toward the sky, Clive's quick thinking took over. He reached into his coat pocket and pulled out a stick of dynamite. With his other hand, he slowly reached into another pocket and fumbled for a match.

Cupping his hand to shield it from the wind, he struck the match against the door. The first attempt failed, but on the second try, the match flared to life. He quickly lit the dynamite's fuse just as the beast locked eyes with him.

As the monster roared, Clive made a desperate move. He jammed his hand, still clutching the dynamite, straight into its gaping mouth. He yanked his arm back as fast as he could while the beast gagged and let out a strangled yelp. Dropping to the floor, Clive crawled beneath the creature's legs and over to Butch, who remained unconscious. He reached his partner just in time before the werewolf exploded, showering them both in blood.

Clive lifted his head, staring at the space where the creature had stood only moments before. The door that had once separated them from the dangers outside was now gone, blown clean off its hinges, leaving a gaping opening for whatever else might be lurking in the darkness.

Turning to Butch, Clive shook him urgently.

"Come on, wake up."

Butch didn't move.

Clive pushed himself up and grabbed the big man by the arms, hooking the lantern's handle between his teeth as he began to drag him toward Jeb's house. He pulled the unconscious man through the debris of dead cattle and scattered werewolf remains until he finally reached the front door. What he wasn't ready for, however, was the sight that awaited him inside.

Clive managed to get Butch safely inside before taking the lantern and looking around. If a house could talk, it would tell one hell of a horror story. Dried blood covered the floor, and overturned chairs lay scattered across the room. This was the place where Ralph had fought with every ounce of strength left in him before he was fatally wounded.

Clive knelt down and ran his fingers across a deep groove in the floor, the very spot where Ralph had managed to drive a knife clean through Jeb's hand, pinning it to the ground.

While examining the room, he heard Butch moan. Clive rushed to him.

"Butch, you alright?"

"Yeah, just hit my head pretty hard against that beam in the barn. Where are we?"

Butch sat up and staggered to his feet. Without question, he was suffering from a concussion.

"Jeb's house," Clive replied.

"What happened to the barn and the monster?"

"I shoved a piece of dynamite down its throat and blew it up. Unfortunately, it took the door out along with it," Clive said, realizing how disturbingly casual his words sounded.

"So, this is that good-for-nothing Jeb's house?"

"Yeah, the son of a bitch looked like he put up a hell of a fight."

Butch bent down and grabbed the pelt Ralph had worn to hide from the werewolves.

"Is that the pelt from the storm cellar?" Clive asked.

"Well, I don't know if anyone else is dumb enough to skin one of those things. Even thinking about it would be a death wish."

"Make sure you bring that back with us. It might actually come in handy. We just need to figure out our next move. I reckon we've got a couple more hours until sunrise, so we'd better come up with something quick."

Just then, the faint creak of a door opening broke the silence, followed by quiet footsteps entering the kitchen.

"Who are you?" a voice asked.

The two men turned toward the doorway to see a woman standing there, prompting them to draw their revolvers and aim them at her.

"Who are you?" Clive demanded.

"Carol Surely, where is my husband?"

"Mrs. Surely, are you aware that there was an attempted murder in this house tonight?"

"Murder? Who? Is Jeb all right?"

The two men holstered their guns. The small woman didn't seem much of a threat, at least not one they couldn't handle together.

"Mrs. Surely, you must have heard the struggle out here this evening."

"My husband came into the room and told me one of those monsters had gotten in and that he needed to handle it. He told me that, no matter what I heard, I was to keep the bedroom door shut. So that is what I did."

"You must have heard the shouts of another man out here," Clive said.

"Oh, Jebby has many friends and business partners coming in and out at all hours of the night. I hear many different voices."

"What about the explosions outside?" Butch chimed in.

"I don't know if you gentlemen have noticed, but there are a lot of crazy things going on outside, so if you think I'm going out there to see, then you are equally crazy. Now, I will ask you again... is Jeb alright?"

"I'm sorry to tell you, Mrs. Surely, but your husband murdered someone this evening and is now deceased."

"You're lying! Jebby was a good man. He would never hurt anyone!" she cried hysterically.

Butch lost his temper and got in her face. "A good man? I'll tell you who a good man is—the man your husband decided to viciously attack in this very house tonight, while you lay in that room and did nothing. The only thing I regret is not killing that waste of skin, Jeb, myself!"

Carol covered her face with her hands and began to cry as Butch stood inches from her. He wore a disgusted look while she sobbed. He finally turned his back to look at Clive, and that was when she made her move. She reached into her dress pocket and pulled out a knife.

"Look out, Butch!" Clive yelled.

Butch turned to Carol as she brought the knife down. He grabbed her left arm and bent it. She began to scream at him.

"Let me go, you murderer!"

She continued to hit him with her right hand. Butch then turned her around and put her in a sleeper hold as she kicked her feet. He tightened the hold to try to calm her, but he was too full of adrenaline to realize he was using too much force. His face turned red from how hard he was squeezing to calm her. That was when he heard a crack, and Carol went limp. His eyes widened in surprise, and he quickly released her. She dropped to the ground and lay motionless.

"Is she knocked out?" he asked, breathing heavily from the struggle.

Clive walked over and flipped her onto her back. He looked for a pulse or to see if her chest was rising to indicate breathing, but found nothing. He shook his head.

"I-I-I didn't mean to. I just wanted her to drop the knife and calm down. You gotta believe me, Clive. I just wanted her to stop."

"I know," Clive said. "Listen, I know you are very upset about what just happened, but we can't stay here."

Butch shook his head, still in disbelief, while Clive thought of a plan to end this night once and for all.

"Do you think we could get our hands on more of those cattle? Maybe we could try the same trick you pulled with the gunpowder."

"I'm afraid that may have been a one-time thing. Even if we cover every animal in Moonlight Valley, there's no guarantee it will lure out every werewolf. Not to mention, if there are more out there, the explosions and the smell of meat might attract even more."

The two stood in silence.

"What's that?" Clive asked.

"What's what?"

"Shhh… that noise. It's very faint."

Ever so quietly, the sound came again. *Choo-choo…*

Butch heard it this time. "Oh, that's the train. It cuts back through here before dawn. Why?"

"The train? That's it!" Clive yelled.

Chapter 21

It Ends Tonight

With mere hours until morning, the two men decided to make the high-risk trip toward the center of town. Knowing that time was of the essence, Clive led the charge with reckless abandon. It was as if the grim reality fueling his fear was, in turn, fueling his fearlessness, a cycle of emotions that fed one another. This was the same man who, earlier that day, had been ready to shut his eyes and accept defeat at the hand of Daniel. Maybe he was saved by Ralph and his crew because his atonement wasn't death. His atonement was to help the four people who had saved him try to stop the hell unleashed in Moonlight Valley from spreading any further.

The journey back into town wasn't as easy as the trip to Jeb's barn. Not far ahead, they saw the shadowy figures of two monsters. Fortunately for them, the beasts had their backs turned, facing town. Clive set the lantern on the ground and let the moonlight guide his steps as he crept within twenty feet of the creatures, walking as softly as he could. Butch had to stay back; being such a large man, his attempt at light steps sounded like normal walking to most.

228

Clive reached into his coat and pulled out another stick of dynamite. He lit the fuse, waited a moment, then hurled it forward so it would explode on impact. *BOOM!* Before the monsters had a chance to realize what hit them, they were blown apart in a cloud of blood and limbs, or so the two men thought.

Clive signaled to Butch that it was safe to move forward. He had cleared the way. Through the limbs and blood-stained ground, Clive hadn't noticed that one of the beasts still had its upper torso intact, allowing it to crawl toward him on its hands while dragging its intestines behind. The creature swiped at Clive and connected, knocking him onto his back. "Ooof!" he grunted as he hit the hard ground. Butch rushed over and drove his knife into the beast's head before it could do any serious damage.

"Maybe we should slow down before running headlong into a town infested with monsters," Butch said in a matter-of-fact tone, handing the lantern back to Clive.

"We don't have much time to slow down."

"Then why did you hear the train's whistle and decide to charge off like a maniac into the night?"

"I'll explain everything when we get back to the jail, but for now, I just need you to trust me. Okay?"

"Alright," Butch replied.

Clive led the way to the jail with the same determination as before, though wearier now, realizing his reckless attitude could cost them not only their plan but also their lives. Butch followed close behind with the pelt tucked under his arm. As they reached the jail door, a bullet whizzed past Clive's head and shattered the window. Both men burst inside and drew their guns. Clive cracked the door open and fired a few shots toward the saloon. Butch took cover to the right of the broken window, crouching behind a wall and occasionally reaching his arm out to fire blindly. A few more shots rang out from the saloon, splintering the jail's walls. After several tense minutes, the shooting finally stopped.

"Alright, you outlaws, come on out," the voice called.

Clive and Butch didn't move.

"You two have caused a real mess this evening, you know that? So come on out, and I might let you live to plead your case to the sheriff tomorrow."

"Sheriff Daniel is one of those monsters now! If we have it our way, he won't see tomorrow!" Clive yelled back.

"I don't know about you, but I have never had the pleasure of meeting Sheriff Daniel. My sheriff is the honorable and just Sheriff Freeman."

"Not another one of these lunatics," Clive muttered to himself.

A man in overalls and a straw hat walked out of the saloon, wielding a rifle.

"Monsters? These beautiful creatures are anything but. In all my days here, I have never seen a creature with purer intentions wanting only to protect its property and the like. People like you see something as beautiful as this, and your first instinct is to scream and shoot. In reality, these noble creatures were here first, and we came and stole their land right out from under them."

"You can't be serious," Butch scoffed.

The man raised his rifle and fired several rounds into the jail. "You outlaws dare poke fun at me? This is exactly what Sheriff Freeman was trying to tell us. People like you come in and try to take our ranching jobs and push us out, leaving us to fight for scraps. You have driven us from our homes just like people drove these defenseless creatures from theirs. Sheriff Freeman told us that what you less-educated folk call werewolves are just our true selves finally bubbling up to claim what is rightfully ours."

Clive opened the jail door and stepped into the doorway with his rifle raised so the man could see him.

"Good," the man said.

"What about the other outlaw?"

Butch moved in front of the broken window and lifted his hands into the air.

"I understand you feel wronged, but you must realize that Dan—Sheriff Freeman has brainwashed you into believing these things are normal. I can't speak to how things were before I arrived, but from what I've seen, nothing about this town is normal. These are flesh-eating monsters. Trust me, I've seen it firsthand."

"There you go with that word again, 'monsters'. Every time people like you see something you don't understand, you label it a monster or an enemy. I can show you firsthand that these creatures are harmless."

Standing on the far side of the train tracks, the man began shouting and firing his rifle into the air. "Hey! I'm right here, come and eat me!" He fired a few more rounds skyward, and to the men's surprise, nothing happened.

"You see, I told you these things aren't monsters, they're just here to take back what is rightfully— AAAHHH!"

Before the man could finish, one of the beasts leapt from the roof of the saloon and crashed down on top of him, crushing him beneath its weight. The man begged the creature to get off, and it did—only to toy with its prey. Unable to stand, the man began to crawl away. The monster stalked after him, nudging him with its nose in cruel mockery. Then it sank its teeth into his back and whipped its head, hurling him high into the air. Out of nowhere, another beast lunged upward and caught him in its jaws. It bolted into the night with the man screaming in agony while the first creature gave chase. It was as if the beasts were playing a grotesque game of keep-away. Clive watched in horror, then slammed the jail door shut.

"How did you know he was going to get attacked by those monsters?" Butch asked.

"The one thing those creatures and Daniel's supporters share is that there's no reasoning with them. Left to their own ways, they always bring about their own downfall."

"Yeah, I guess if someone thinks those monsters are friendly creatures, then it's only a matter of time before they do something stupid like that."

The train whistle grew louder, indicating it was getting closer. "We don't have much time. We need to get to the basement quickly," Clive said.

"Why?"

"Down there is how we finish this once and for all."

The two made their way downstairs with lanterns in hand. "That's our solution right there."

"What is?" Butch asked, growing more annoyed that Clive wouldn't just say it.

"Open your eyes, man. The mountain of explosives right in front of us. We bring all these boxes of gunpowder and dynamite and leave them on the tracks."

"Are you out of your mind? First of all, trying to lug all of this outside with those things attacking everything in sight is a death wish for sure."

"You have the pelt upstairs, don't you?"

"Even if we're able to bring all these crates outside before the train passes through, the explosion will wipe out the whole town. Nothing will be left."

Clive put his hand on Butch's shoulder. "Butch, I know you hate to admit it, but there isn't anything left of this town. I know you love it, but you're in love with what it was. I'm sorry to say there's no going back to that anymore. Everyone you loved has either become one of those monsters or bought into Daniel's bullshit. To put it bluntly, the infection has gotten so bad that we have to cut off the limb. We need to warn other towns that Daniel may have sent monsters their way before they, too, become infested."

The big man was overwhelmed with emotion. "I'm sorry… I can't do that."

"Butch, I know Moonlight Valley is your home, but—"

"No, that isn't it," Butch said, hemming and hawing as he tried to get the words out.

He opened his hands to reveal teeth marks on his palms.

"B-Butch, what's that?"

"It happened back in the storage room of the saloon. When I snapped the monster's jaw, I must have pressed so hard on its teeth that it broke the skin. At first, I thought it didn't matter because so much time had passed, and I didn't feel any different. That was until the incident with Jeb's wife. I knew I should have let go, but something inside me told me to squeeze tighter. I think because it was such a minor bite and I'm such a big man, the reaction was delayed. I can't go with you to warn others, but I can stay and go down with the town I love."

Clive began to cry and hugged Butch. The whistle from the train grew louder, and the two knew they needed to act immediately. They worked as quickly as they could to carry the mountain of explosives from the basement up to the main floor of the jail. Once completed, Butch donned the pelt and gave Clive one final nod of respect before heading for the door.

"Oh no!" Clive said, a sudden realization hitting him.

"What?"

"There's someone driving the train. We can't let them plow into the explosives; they'd die for sure. I can't have another innocent person die tonight."

"What are you suggesting?"

"Do you think Daniel's horse is still locked up in the stable out back?"

"I mean, unless one of the beasts got into it, I don't see why it wouldn't be."

Clive handed Butch the revolver with one silver bullet left, and off he went out the jail door toward the back. Clive was lucky enough not to run into any werewolves on the way and found the stable still locked. He shot the lock with his revolver, gained access to the stall, mounted Daniel's horse, and rode off. Clive rode hard toward the train, its headlight just beginning to glow at the edge of town. He knew he needed to ride as fast as possible to catch it in time. However, a few of the beasts noticed him and were hot on his tail.

The werewolves were so fast that, at one point, Clive couldn't tell if the pounding in his chest was his own heartbeat or the thunder of their footsteps closing in. He glanced back and could have sworn he saw one lunge over the others, desperate to claim the prize first.

After a stretch of riding, most of the monsters fell back, deciding the massive train was the greater predator. All but one. One beast made it his mission to reach Clive before he could make it to the train.

The whistle shrieked, the headlight now only feet away, but the beast didn't falter. Clive knew that once he cleared the front of the train, he'd need to turn and ride parallel, matching its speed. He approached from the left, drawing closer and closer. Then he made a split-second decision, one that could cost him his life, and, if he failed, condemn the poor train driver to die when the locomotive reached town and struck the explosives.

Clive dashed across the tracks at the last second, veering to the right side of the train. Had he waited a heartbeat longer, he would have been crushed beneath it. Unfortunately, the werewolf wasn't so lucky. When it dove across the tracks in pursuit, the train struck it head-on, obliterating the creature on impact.

Clive wheeled his horse around and pushed hard to catch the front of the locomotive. Once alongside, he did everything he could to get the conductor's attention. Realizing it was no use, he knew he would have to jump aboard and pull the man off himself. He lined up the horse with the engine, steadied his breath, and leapt.

He landed on the engine and shouted at the conductor, "You need to get off! There's an accident ahead!"

The terrified conductor, thinking he was being robbed, tried to reason with Clive.

"No, you need to get off!" Clive barked.

But the man wasn't about to surrender his train, so Clive forced the issue, grabbing him and hurling him from the cab. Luckily, the horse was still galloping alongside, and the conductor managed to seize the reins, saving himself from injury.

Once inside the cab, the realization of what Clive had to do struck him as hard as the train had struck the werewolf. To keep the speed necessary to set off the explosives, someone had to stay aboard and drive the locomotive straight through. That was when Clive understood his purpose in all of this, why he had been dragged into this cursed town, why his life had been spared from the noose that very morning.

Deep down, he knew he should have been hanged for his past actions. He wasn't a religious man, but he prayed that if there was life after all of this, he might have a chance to make peace. He would genuinely offer his apologies to the man back in Dodge City and to Paul and Susan Kelp. He would look Ralph in the eyes and say, "Thank you. We did it, pal."

Meanwhile, back at the jail, Butch dragged the crates of explosives out to the tracks, still cloaked in the werewolf pelt. As he lifted the last crate, the revolver holding the silver bullet slipped from his waistband and clattered, unseen, to the floor. Butch, unaware, pressed on. He was nearly finished when Daniel, the massive, hulking beast, appeared and attacked.

Daniel loomed over the crates of explosives, tilting his head like a curious dog before throwing back his snout and unleashing a deafening howl. Butch dropped the crate he carried and bolted for the jail. The sound of the fall caught Daniel's attention, and the monster turned on him. With a savage lunge, Daniel's claws tore the pelt clean off. Butch's hands shot to his waistband, desperate for the revolver that could end Daniel's reign of terror once and for all, but his fingers grasped only empty air.

It was as if the beast knew what he was searching for. Daniel bared his razor-sharp teeth in a mocking grin, savoring Butch's misfortune.

Butch sighed and reached for the revolver at his hip. He knew it wouldn't kill Daniel, but it might at least slow him down. He fired once, the bullet tearing into the monster's shoulder and drawing a roar of pain. He fired again, this time striking its leg. Before he could pull the trigger a third time, the beast swiped the revolver clean from his hand.

Daniel's massive, wolf-like paws clamped around Butch, lifting him as though he were weightless, then hurling him through the air. He crashed onto the tracks in front of the mountain of explosives, the breath torn from his lungs by the impact of the iron rails. Gasping, he looked up to see the monster stalking closer, savoring each deliberate step.

Daniel threw back his head and howled at the fading moon before lowering his gaze to Butch. He loomed over him, drool dripping onto Butch's face. Razor-sharp claws sank into his shoulders, pinning him down, leaving no chance of escape. This was the moment Daniel had waited for, vengeance against the man and his crew who had ruined his plans for domination.

Face-to-face with Butch, who writhed in agony beneath him, the beast prepared to finish it. And then, from the distance, came a hoarse, exhausted voice:

"Hey, Daniel… This is for Moonlight Valley."

The monster turned toward the doorway of the jail, where Ralph stood slumped against the frame, his body smeared with blood. In his hand was the revolver Butch had dropped earlier. With the last of his strength, Ralph raised the gun and fired the final silver bullet at Daniel.

The beast's eyes widened as the shot cut through the air, seeming to move in slow motion. The bullet flew and just barely missed its mark. "No," Ralph rasped, his voice torn and broken, before collapsing to the ground and exhaling his final breath.

Daniel's lips curled into a cruel grin as he glanced at Ralph's lifeless body, then turned his gaze back to Butch. That was it, the last desperate attempt to stop him had failed. By tomorrow, he would revert to his human form and rule Moonlight Valley with an iron fist.

But Daniel had grown too consumed with tormenting his prey to notice the massive train bearing down on the stockpile of explosives.

The collision came with such force that the town and the surrounding mile erupted in a storm of fire. Buildings disintegrated in an instant, reduced to rubble and ash. The once-thriving Moonlight Valley, a place settlers had risked everything to call home, became a graveyard for those desperate to escape.

In the aftermath, sheriffs from neighboring towns would dismiss it all as a tragic train accident. By the time the sun rose, no one would remember Moonlight Valley. No voices would remain to tell the horror of what had transpired there.

The next day in Dodge City, the sun blazed high overhead as townsfolk carried on with their routines. Ranchers tended cattle, banks opened their doors, and the air buzzed with the restless energy of a hot July afternoon.

Inside the saloon, men sat hunched over a poker table, cards shuffling and chips clinking. When the game finally ended, the players set their hands down. A sharply dressed man leaned forward with a smooth grin and said, "Why don't we play another, gentlemen? The game's called Three-Card Monte. Allow me to introduce myself—the name's Ed."